Charles L. Youngblood

A Mighty Hunter

The adventures of Charles L. Youngblood on the plains and mountains

Charles L. Youngblood

A Mighty Hunter
The adventures of Charles L. Youngblood on the plains and mountains

ISBN/EAN: 9783337317355

Printed in Europe, USA, Canada, Australia, Japan

Cover: Foto ©Andreas Hilbeck / pixelio.de

More available books at **www.hansebooks.com**

A MIGHTY HUNTER.

THE ADVENTURES OF
CHARLES L̶ ̶ ̶ ̶NGBLOOD ON THE
PLAI̶ ̶ ̶ ̶ MOUNTAINS.

MR. ̶ ̶ ̶ ̶ JOURNAL.

PROFUSELY ILLUSTR̶ ̶ ̶

CHICAGO AND NEW YORK
RAND, MCNALLY & COMPANY, PUBLISHE̶ ̶ ̶

1890.

TO MY AGED FATHER,

WHOSE PATERNAL CARE AND AFFECTION HAVE BEEN SO

CONSTANTLY MANIFESTED TOWARD ME

DURING MY WHOLE LIFE,

THIS BOOK IS AFFECTIONATELY DEDICATED.

C. L. Y.

CONTENTS.

(7)

8 CONTENTS.

10 CONTENTS.

CHAPTER XXIV.

CHAPTER I.

INTRODUCTION.

The days of the lordly bison are numbered. Here and there, in the far Northwest, a solitary estray, which has thus far escaped its inevitable doom, is encountered by the red or the white hunter, but altogether there are scarcely enough left to yield one specimen to each of the zoölogical gardens of the country. It was not so, however, in the '60s, when the subject of this narrative migrated from his home in Indiana to the great plains. At that time, countless herds of buffalo shook the solid earth with their mighty trampling, and no one would have credited the tremendous slaughter that was to be accomplished in the next quarter of a century.

Let us, then, ere the bison passes into the annals of mythology, and he that has seen a buffalo is laughed at as a relater of fairy tales,

record the adventures of a hunter of those
powerful and formidable beasts.

Charles L. Youngblood was born in Ander-
son Township, Warrick County, Indiana, on
the 9th of April, 1826. His father was a
Methodist minister, a native of South Caro-
lina, and his mother was a Virginian. The
first forty years of Charles' life were devoted
to farming, and during those years he
learned, if not much from books, a vast deal
from Nature. His education was of the most
rudimentary sort, for it was not until years
later that the modern pedagogue, with his
globes, and his charts, and his thousand and
one devices for teaching the young idea how
to shoot, got abroad in the land. The
Hoosier school-house of those days was a
primitive log cabin, with a big open fire-
place, wherein the great logs roared, and
snapped, and sizzled during the three or four
winter months which constituted the school
session; and the presiding genius was a sort
of bugaboo, whose rod backed the infallible
authority of the blue-covered spelling-book,

and concealed only too often the scant limits of his own information. Country life, in those days, was generous, spontaneous, and free, and all men were neighbors on the principle of the golden rule, for occasions often rose when a friendly neighbor was about the handiest thing a man could have about him. It has been frequently noted that life in the country is far more sociable than that of a city, and the observation might be formulated in a general rule, that the farther apart the houses the closer together are the hearts. Innumerable occasions for social gatherings were known to our fathers which we, in these populous times, have never known. There were log-rollings, quilting-bees, wood-chopping matches, camp-meetings (real *camp*-meetings they were, too, and not the pretenses of to-day), corn-huskings, and affairs of that sort, which kept dwellers at a distance neighborly and familiar; and to the old settler who compares the selfish rush and scramble of our times with the friendly generosity of the days of his youth, it must appear that the world has lost something in becoming more thrifty and enlightened.

Perhaps it was a sense of the decay of primitive customs, coupled with an innate love for adventure, which caused the young farmer, whose historian we are, to weary of his Indiana home, and to follow, with longing eyes, the westward course of the nation's eager, pulsing life.

Some men are born to be pioneers; the conventionalities and tame monotony of civilized life are irksome to them, and in all places, except upon the frontiers, where life is a rough-and-tumble sport with the elements, they are dissatisfied and out of place. Youngblood was such an one, and in 1865 his longing for the free, open life of the backwoods became so strong and keen, that he cut abruptly loose from the ties of friends and kindred, and, with his wife and children, started out on the western trail, across Illinois and Missouri, and brought up in Kansas City, which, at that period, was nothing but a small frontier town, with a convenient location upon the Kansas-Missouri State line. The pioneer had reached the frontier once more, and, thenceforward, he never turned back to, nor regretted, the civilization he had abandoned. Fortunately, for those who have done, and will do, the same, some men are "built that way."

CHAPTER II.

When Youngblood reached Kansas City,
in 1865, the "boom" had not yet struck the
town, and it was a small, uninviting,
unpromising place. The new-comer had
almost money enough in his pocket to buy
it as it stood, and still have enough left
to make some of the improvements which
it sadly needed. In the light of later developments, he has been bitterly sorry that
he did not. If the struggling town had
looked more inviting, he might now be
the landlord of about 200,000 tenants; but
the miserable, squalid shanties of that day
he had no use for, and later, when he
wanted to buy, the owners were not in a
trading humor. Accordingly, he lingered
but a short time in the embryo metropolis of

the Southwest, ere he pushed on into Kansas. But, in spite of his frontiersman-like tendencies, accustomed as he had grown to ten-acre fields with neat fences about them, the broad, open, treeless prairies seemed desolate indeed; so, in despair, the pioneer retraced his steps into Missouri, where he finally bought a farm near the center of the State, and remained there until 1870.

While living here, the "boom" came along, and, in its impetuous rush, struck Mr. Youngblood several severe blows. A railroad was surveyed through the section in which his farm was situated, and a town laid out—on paper. It was a "dead sure thing;" work was already begun on the railroad, and town lots were bound to command a premium as soon as the line reached the place. It was too good a chance to be missed, with millions sticking out of it at every corner; so Mr. Youngblood laid out several thousands of dollars in buying up a good part of the town from the misguided owners, who were sacrificing the land at about ten times its real value. Soon afterward, history once more demonstrated its parrot-like ways of repetition, the projected railway fell through, and the man who was to have prospered by the now collapsed "boom," found it hard to unburden himself of his superfluous real estate, even at prices that amounted to a virtual giving of it away. The speculator had greater reason than ever to regret that he had not purchased Kansas City, but still more that he had bought a city which was "bound to grow."

Disheartened at this unlucky turn of the wheel, Mr. Youngblood once more pulled up stakes and again turned his face toward the setting sun, with a cargo consisting of about 200 bushels of dried fruit and a lot of butter. He passed through Denver, Golden City, Black Hawk City, and Central City to Nevada City, where he sold out his cargo and cast about for an anchorage.

Nevada City, at this time, was herself enjoying a "boom," a genuine "boom." The mining fever was at its height, and everyone was infected and drawn into the mad rush after wealth. The town was young and typically frontier. Everybody had something to do, and did it, and it was as impossible to escape the excitement as it would have been to get rich by sitting down and waiting for a ship to sail down the mountains. But while the larger proportion of the populace were seeking the elusive metals, others, with wise forethought, calculated that while "pay dirt" might or might not be struck, it was certain that where people are congregated there will money be spent, and so they set themselves about securing that wealth that was not problematical. Among other odd industries practiced with this end in view, the novel scheme of poultry-raising excited our new settler's curiosity. At the very first, it did not strike him as very much of a business, in fact, he considered it as about as close to nothing as an enterprise could come; but inquiry developed the fact that the poultry-rancher was not so devoid of understanding, after all. The

ranch was about five miles from the mines,
where thousands of miners, with full-grown
appetites, were at work, and in the immediate
neighborhood were several immense boarding-
houses, some of them patronized by as many
as 1,500 boarders. In these great eating-
houses the poultry-raiser found a ready and

profitable demand for the entire product of
his ranch, and obtained from them, simply
at the trouble of carrying the stuff away,
table-scraps that reduced his feed-bill to
absolutely nothing. He was getting at the
time from 50 cents to $1.00 apiece for chickens,
and about as much a dozen for eggs, of which

he was selling some ninety dozens daily. He owned about 2,000 hens, and, having a monopoly of the business, with light labor and small expense, was making money hand over fist.

But Youngblood, after maturely considering the matter, decided that he did not come so far simply to open a hen-house, and looked further.

One day, as he was wandering through the town on the lookout for an opening, he passed a house before which a large crowd had collected.

"What's up?" he asked of a bystander.

"Man chawed up by a cinnamon b'ar," was the curt response.

Youngblood entered the house, and saw the poor unfortunate stretched on a lounge awaiting death. But he was an old hunter, and "game" to his last breath; and, seeing the stranger's interest, described the fight, while the death-dew was gathering on his brow.

It seemed that he had shot and badly wounded the bear, and was following its trail through a rocky piece of underbrush, when suddenly he came face to face with the enraged brute. Before, in his surprise, he had time to raise his rifle, the bear sprang upon him and dashed him to the ground. They rolled together over and over among the rocks, until, in his frantic efforts to free himself, both the man's legs were broken. Realizing that further struggle would be useless, he resorted to strategy, and lay perfectly still, feigning death. The bear released his embrace, and, after eyeing and smelling him suspiciously for a few moments, turned and started slowly and heavily away. As soon as his antagonist had gone a few feet off, the man raised himself painfully on his hands and knees, and began to crawl away; but the slight noise he was forced to make attracted the bear's attention, and it sprang upon him again with redoubled fury, breaking one of his wrists. He again had recourse to the same strategy, and with more success this time, as he remained motionless until the animal was out of sight, and then began dragging

himself homeward through the snow, which
was about four inches deep.

A few moments after the encounter, his
brother happening to pass that way, noticed
the marks of the struggle, and, following the
bloody trail in the snow, soon came up with
the wounded bear, which turned fiercely
upon him, eager for another fight. But a
repeating rifle soon placed the brute *hors de
combat*, and the victor turned back to find
the other party to the fight. Following the
trail for about half a mile, he finally came
up with the wounded man, and his feelings
can better be imagined than described on
recognizing in the mutilated being his own
brother. The poor fellow, with one wrist
and both legs broken, had dragged himself
that distance over the rocks and through the
snow. He was carried to the nearest house,
where Youngblood heard his story, and
where he died, after lingering a few hours in
mortal agony. His grief-stricken father
made a vow over the dead body of his son,
that he would have the bear skinned and

would sleep upon its hide as long as he lived.

This grim incident made a decided impression upon Youngblood, in fact, decided him to become a hunter, and an opportunity to begin his new vocation soon presented itself.

A few days later, at Golden City, he fell in with a party of hunters who were on the eve of starting on a big buffalo-hunt, and Youngblood seized with avidity upon the chance to have some sport, and, at the same time, make a little money; for buffalo-hunting, be it well understood, was a very profitable business, the cured meat being readily disposed of and the hides commanding good figures.

The hunters welcomed the new-comer to their ranks, and with great satisfaction he began his preparations.

But before the expedition started, a little mischance came very near putting our friend in the town jail instead of on the plains. In order to dry out his gun, he loaded it one day with a charge of powder and fired it at random through the front door of his dwelling. A moment afterward, he was surprised at the sight of a policeman, who ran across the street, and, taking him by the arm, said:

"Come along with me, sir! That is against the law." At this, Youngblood quickly made up his mind that he was in a bad strait, and decided to try the effect of stupidity upon the guardian of the peace; so, assuming a look of innocent surprise, he said:

"Why, what's wrong, mister? I hain't done nothin'."

"Oh! you haven't, haven't you?" exclaimed the policeman. "Didn't you shoot into the public street?"

"Sho!" ejaculated Youngblood, "you ain't a goin' to take me up jest fer firin' off a load of powder fer fun, are you?"

"Yes, it's against the law, and you'll have to come along with me."

"I didn't know that," said Youngblood. "Ef I'd a knowed that, you bet I wouldn't ha' done it. Can't you let me off this time?" .

While the policeman was considering the

matter, the town marshal, who had been aroused by the shooting, came up, and quickly recognizing in the prisoner a brother Mason, accepted his excuse, and, advising him to be more careful in the future, set him free. Thereafter, when he wished to dry out his gun, he used a swab.

CHAPTER III.

OUT FOR A HUNT—A MISSING OVERCOAT.—
YOUNGBLOOD'S FIRST BUFFALO—INDIANS
ON THE TRAMP—OLD POISON-SLINGER, ETC.

The preparations for his first expedition as
a hunter were soon made, and, in company
with three other men, all accomplished
scouts, Youngblood set out from Golden
City on an eighty-mile tramp after buffalo.
The first game they struck was a herd of
antelope, of which they succeeded in bagging one. After this little triumph, they
pressed on for about a mile farther, when
they stumbled upon a dug-out, where they
resolved to pass the night. After some parley, they proposed to the owner of the primitive dwelling that they pay for their
accommodations with antelope-meat, which
bargain was struck then and there.

Congratulating themselves upon the
" dicker," they slept soundly that night, but

by the next morning their enterprising landlord had changed his mind and demanded
$5.00 for his hospitality. This seemed very
mean; but the money was finally paid,
not, however, without value received. Their
host had entertained them the night before
by displaying a new overcoat, which he
had just bought for $14.00. He never
enjoyed the luxurious warmth of that coat,
for when his guests bade him farewell, it
somehow managed to keep them company.
It was a good trade—$5.00 for a $14.00
overcoat, and they all got the worth of their
money, for, being a community purchase,
they wore the garment turn and turn about.

Pushing forward, without any qualms of
conscience, they reached a spot that promised
good hunting. They were confident, from
various signs well known to Youngblood's
companions, that there was game in the
vicinity, but were at a loss how to get at it,
as there was no timber at hand in which to
conceal themselves. It was a wide, treeless
stretch of prairie, and the buffalo would

have seen them miles away. However, they
determined to go into camp. Youngblood
was wild to catch his first glimpse of the big

game; so, leaving his companions to make
the preparations for camping, he stole away
by himself, struck off from the road, and

after a walk of several miles, his hopes were realized by the sight of a large herd of bison. His heart beat high with excitement, but he kept at a respectful distance from them for two reasons: first, because, being a novice, he was somewhat frightened by the great, shaggy, heaving mass of ·horned life, and, second, because he feared that he in his turn might alarm them. However, keeping himself carefully concealed, he crept gradually closer, and when within about 500 yards, aimed at the herd and fired. It was something like the traditional shot at the barn-door, but it scored, and he enjoyed the supreme satisfaction of seeing his first buffalo go down. He was so elated with the success of this, his virgin effort, that, though he might easily have dropped a dozen, he contented himself with self-congratulation, and hurried back as fast as his legs could carry him to receive the congratulations of his friends.

The entire party then turned out to bring the trophy into camp.

But Youngblood's adventures for the day were not yet at an end; for, on their way to the place where the slain monster lay, a huge bull was spied, heading almost directly for the party. "What man has done, man can do," reasoned the doughty nimrod, and he begged his companions to allow him to try his hand alone at this monarch of the prairie. Their consent somewhat reluctantly obtained, he moved a short distance to one side, and lay down directly in the path of the approaching animal. On came the unwieldy brute, and when the bloodshot whites of his eyes were visible, a somewhat close range, the concealed hunter fired. A tuft of wool flew from the bison's back, but he charged straight on in an unswerving line. In a flash, another cartridge was inserted, and again Youngblood fired. But it had no apparent effect on the bull, except to irritate him, and to show him the enemy that had stung him. He had not paid much attention to the first shot, but the second he evidently regarded as an insult, and, lowering his

3

head, came thundering right upon the now thoroughly frightened hunter, who began to think that hunting the buffalo was not such fun, after all, and to wonder whether the beast, when infuriated, attacks with its hoofs, its horns, or its teeth, or with all three, when, to his infinite relief, the animal dropped dead in its tracks, within a few yards of him.

For the next few hours, Youngblood fancied that he could teach the rest all about the business, and when, a short time after, he sighted a herd about a mile distant, he started off to put his theories into practice.

He got within range and fired, killing one, when immediately the entire herd gathered about it, bellowing and tossing their heads in consternation. Here was his chance, and he kept blazing away until he had dispatched eight and driven the rest of the herd away.

That settled it, and he regarded himself as a whole "Wild West Combination"— Indians and cow-boys included.

The carcasses were quickly dressed, and the party started on their return to camp. They had retraced their steps but a short distance, when they perceived a large band of Indians approaching. It was an anxious moment, and caused them not a little trepidation until they discovered that the red brothers were not on the war-path. The band numbered about 1,500, and they had a permit from the Government to hunt for thirty days. It was a strange and novel sight to the man fresh from civilization, and he watched the procession curiously as it filed past. First came the warriors on their ponies, and after them a straggling line of squaws and luggage. The pappooses were lashed on the backs of ponies, which were turned loose and driven like a herd of cows. After the manner of the noble "Lo," all the work was left to the squaws, who drove the laden pack-horses, and looked after the luggage and pappooses, while the chivalrous warriors rode at their ease on ahead.

The weather was piercing cold, and the

driving snow pelted the unprotected faces of
the pappooses, but they were toughened,
and took it as a matter of course, laughing
and crowing with delight, while their small
eyes glittered like black beads. Some of the
youngest of them were carried in a sort of
pocket, made by slinging a blanket between
two poles, to one end of which a horse was
harnessed as to a pair of shafts, while the
other end dragged upon the ground. It
made a primitive but efficient perambulator,
and the babies appeared to enjoy it. As the
long procession filed past, one of the ponies
shied violently at the strangers, made a dash
and jumped across a narrow gulch, causing
some excitement, and slinging out the little
fellows it carried, like young birds tipped
out of a nest. Youngblood's acquaintance
with Indians and Indian characteristics was
afterward considerable, but this was the only
time he ever knew an Indian, young or old,
to shed tears.

The slain bison were safely brought into
camp, but buffalo-meat, at this time, was a

drug in the market, and it did not pay to
save it, so for the remainder of the expedition Youngblood and his companions went
hunting simply for the sake of the hides.
They were very successful, and in a few days
they had killed over 100, all of which they
carefully skinned, leaving the carcasses to
rot upon the plains.

While out on this, his first hunt, our friend
met with a decidedly painful accident. As
he was pushing his way into camp after a long
tramp across the prairie, he saw three buffalo
lying down. He had only five cartridges
left; so, to make sure of them, he slipped up
as close as he could, and then fired, killing
two and mortally wounding the other. His
last cartridge, with which he meant to put an
end to the injured survivor, failed to fire,
and as he was attempting to pick it out, it
exploded, frightfully mangling his hand.
This accident prevented all hunting for
nearly two weeks, and came very near being
the cause of a still greater misfortune.

While his hand was still too sore to handle

a gun, he had wandered out by himself, and, at some distance from the camp, was strolling leisurely along a branch, when, attracted by an unusual rustling sound, he happened to look up, and over the top of a ridge, only a few yards away, he saw the "tips" of several Indians, as they passed in single file on the other side. Unarmed as he was, his heart was in his mouth, for he recognized them as belonging to a hostile tribe. With great presence of mind, and as noiselessly as possible, he threw himself flat on his face, and, with great good luck, the Indians passed without observing him, for, if he had attracted their attention, they would certainly have made short work of him. This was a lesson to him, and in the future he never went far from the camp without his trusty "old poison-slinger," which was the picturesque name given his gun by his companions.

"Old poison-slinger" was a Sharp's rifle, 50-caliber, made to load and shoot eight times a minute, and capable of throwing a ball to kill at a distance of five miles.

Youngblood often killed with it buffalo which were a mile away, and made such long shots with it that, after firing, he had plenty of time to raise his head and mark the ball as it struck its goal.

Not long after the accident to Youngblood's hand, two of the hunters decided that they had had enough of it, and returned home; but by this time our hero had become enthusiastic in regard to the sport, and he managed to persuade the third man to remain awhile longer. This man was a most excellent shot, and the two hit it off very well together.

On one occasion, when they were out shooting, about twenty miles back from their camp, close to a little stream, which bore the grewsome name of Cold Hell Creek, Youngblood's partner had a good chance to prove his ability as a shot, and by so doing, in all probability, saved his own life. He had killed several buffalo, and wounded one cow, which fell over on its side. The hunter advanced to kill, but before he had come very close to her, fortunately for him, she

beyond their most sanguine expectations.
As they were riding along one morning, disheartened and discouraged at their ill-suc-
cess, there suddenly burst upon their
entranced view the most tremendous herd
of the longed-for beasts that Youngblood had
ever seen in his life, or, in his long and varied
experience, ever saw again. It was impossible to form any conjecture of how far east
or west the vast mass extended. On it came,
like an enormous dark, whirling cloud, and
with a mighty thunder of hoofs that shook
the plain as if it had been riven by an earth-
quake, frightening the horses so that they
became almost unmanageable, and electrify-
ing both men to the highest pitch of excitement. All that day, and all that night, in a
broad column, the great animals tramped by
with a heavy, continual rumble, and an
incessant bellowing. No thought of sleep
came to the sportsmen, even if sleep had
been possible in the midst of the uproar.
One continual blaze of fire sprang from their
guns, and when the herd had passed, the

number of carcasses amounted to 103, which would have been even much larger if they had not paused occasionally to remove the skins of those they had already killed.

They returned to their camp, elated beyond all description, but full of wonderment as to what could be the cause of such a large herd passing at full gallop. Their curiosity was finally satisfied, for they found out some time afterward that trouble had broken out between the Cheyenne Indians and the Utes, and the Utes, being beaten and driven back, had set fire to the prairie to prevent pursuit. This conflagration in the high, thick grass had, in its spread, driven before it the buffalo, antelope, wolves, and other four-footed denizens of the great plains.

With this magnificent result closed the first experience of the young emigrant from Hoosierdom in his new career, which he afterward pursued with constant delight to himself, and an ever-increasing prosperity to his pocket.

CHAPTER IV.

BAD INDIANS—BUFFALO CHIPS—A FRIGHT-
ENED HUNTER—NOT QUITE DEAD YET,
ETC.

After the extraordinary prowess which
Youngblood had exhibited, even in his
novitiate, he felt, and justly, that he should
no longer be reckoned as a "tenderfoot," but ·
was entitled to take his position as a full-
fledged hunter and scout. But thus early in
his career he was condemned to meet with
one rather serious drawback to the safe and
successful pursuit of his vocation. One of
the periodical Indian outbreaks occurred, and
the Indians became so aggressive that hunters
were compelled, for their own security, to go
out in squads of from eight to a score, and
even then their excursions were attended with
considerable risk.

Almost every day the killing of one or
more hunters was reported. These were

generally solitary scouts, for the Indians are
usually far too cowardly to make an attack,
unless their own numbers are overwhelm-
ingly the greater. The plan which meets
with the most favor among these aborigines
is for a large band to creep about and surround a small party of three or four whites,
and then, with fiendish delight, shoot down
the defenseless men or put them to death
with the most horribly ingenious tortures.

It was not long before Youngblood had
some experience of their treacherous double-
dealing. He was one of a band of ten buffalo-
hunters, when a troop of Ogallahs encamped
not far from them. They had come from
their own reservation with the usual thirty
days' hunting permit from Uncle Sam. One
day, soon after their arrival in the vicinity,
a small squad rode over to the white men's
camp. They appeared friendly enough, and,
after some preliminary talk, proposed to race
the horses they rode with those of the
hunters, the winners in the several races to
take both horses. The Indians were unlucky,

and to a man lost their mounts. Then they put up their guns, but with no better success. They bore their losses with stolidity, however, and did not seem much chagrined, but shook hands all around with the greatest appearance of good-will. In fact, their professions of friendship were so profuse that the suspicions of Youngblood and his friends were strongly aroused, and they became very uneasy, knowing, as they did, if the redskins should prove revengeful, they were no match for them in numbers. They determined, therefore, to take all precautions possible. They tethered the horses close together in a bunch, devoured a hasty supper, saw that their weapons were all in fighting trim, and then put out the fire and laid down, but not to sleep. They were on the watch and prepared for the attack that they felt confident was certain to come.

Nor were their premonitions destined to prove untrue. For a time all was quiet, but about two hours after dark, here and there a form was discovered by the sharp eyes of the hunters, creeping stealthily toward their camp. Their object was evidently to get back their own horses, steal as many of the others as they could, and, in case of discovery, to massacre the whole party before they should recover from their surprise. But they had to deal with men who knew their ways well, and who could be quite as cunning as themselves should the circumstances demand.

The little party of watchers waited until the would-be thieves, and possible murderers, were as close as they considered they ought to come, and then, at a low word of command, opened fire upon them with their repeating rifles. This was wholly unexpected to the Indians, as they were certain the whole camp was buried in sleep. It was a decided case of the biter bit, and, with wild yells of rage and execration, all those who had escaped scathless from the bullets took to their heels and ran as fast as their legs could carry them. A few of the hunters sprang to their feet and pursued them, but only a short dis-

tance, as they did not care to come into conflict with the large force not far away.

There was not much sleep for the white
men that night, and the next day they
decided it would be best to remain in camp,
for they knew well that they had not heard
the last of the little affair of the previous
night, but would be obliged to make some
kind of a settlement with the enraged and
outwitted Ogallahs. Sure enough, before 10
o'clock in the morning, a large body of them
were seen slowly approaching the camp. It
must be borne in mind that the noble savage
is Uncle Sam's particular pet, and the hunters
would not dare to lift a single finger unless
they were attacked. But, in view of this
last contingency, they had gotten everything
in readiness, and were on the alert and prepared for any emergency that might arise by
the time the Indians were within speaking
distance.

The chief, who spoke fair, not to say idio-
matically emphatic, English, cried out explo-
sively:

4

"You d—d—— —— ——killed four of my men out there!"

As he spoke, he waved his hand to where lay four bodies of dead Ogallahs.

One of the hunters, Hank Miller by name, replied, "Pawnees!" meaning that the men had been killed by the Pawnees. At this the old chief flew into a violent passion, and roared out: "Pawnees! no Pawnees!" at the same time drawing his finger in a rapid circle about his head to indicate that, had the killing been done by the Pawnees, they would have scalped their victims, which, of course, the white men had not done. "Pawnees! Pooh! Pooh! Pooh!" he repeated, with a world of utter disbelief expressed in the ejaculation.

For some little while the chief and his braves sat upon their horses and bandied words with their pale brethren, all the time watching very closely for any relaxation of vigilance that might give them the opportunity of comparatively safe attack they longed for. But the wary hunters were too much for them. They stood erect and watchful, with their guns in their hands, their thumbs on the hammers, and their fingers on the trigger. They could have fired at a second's notice, and, all being dead shots, each one would, undoubtedly, have killed his man. The Indians were quite well aware of this, and seeing that any plan of retaliation they had formed was wholly unfeasible, they finally rode away, muttering imprecations on their too cunning foes as they disappeared. This was the end of the trouble, however. The hunters were not disturbed any further, and returned peacefully to their hunting for the rest of the thirty days, killing on an average 100 buffalo a day.

After this hunt was over, Youngblood decided to return for a time to Missouri. After remaining there for about six months, his roving instincts and a desperate longing for the excitement of the chase got the better of him, and he once more started West.

Before leaving Missouri, however, he made arrangements with two inhabitants of Warrensburg, A. Buckmaster and L. S. Shidler, to dispose of the meat he should send to them; and he also induced two Missourians, Louis Allred and Silas McFerrin, to accompany him on his expedition.

After traveling some fourteen days they came to a place where there was every prospect of "good hunting." Buffalo abounded, and without any difficulty Youngblood succeeded in bagging an average of eight a day. The hides and flesh of eight good buffalo brought at least $50 in the market, and so he was making a most excellent thing of it, as well as enjoying capital sport.

They had pitched their camp on the banks of a little stream, known as the Sappy River. The country was flat and open, and it was at least twenty miles from any timber. During their sojourn here, they were overtaken by a heavy snow-storm, the snow falling to a depth of over a foot on a level, and Youngblood and his two companions were obliged to remain shut up in their tent for three days, with scarcely any fuel, the storm having

come on so suddenly that they were prevented from laying in a supply. They had
only a very small amount on hand, and that
consisted almost exclusively of buffalo chips,
which is simply the excrement of the buffalo
dried in the sun.

This, to the uninitiated, would probably
seem a very poor substitute for coal or wood,
but in the Far West it is preferred to anything else for all ordinary purposes. Much
hotter fires can be made from it than that
produced by wood. Easterners would probably feel considerable delicacy in using
such fuel, but the wives of the pioneers think
nothing of carrying a load of it in their
aprons, and in almost every house a sackful
of it can be found standing in a corner, and
when the fire needs replenishing, the mistress
of the house takes a few chips from the sack
and throws them on the fire with no more
compunction than if she were handling wood
or coal. By a careful use of their buffalo
chips, the three companions contrived to
escape freezing, and when the snow had dis-

appeared, they prepared to resume their hunting.

The actual hunting itself, however, was confined to Youngblood himself, for neither Allred nor McFerrin, the two men he had brought with him, were in the least skilled in the noble sport. He had employed them simply to skin and prepare the meat of the buffalo after his own gun had brought them low. Allred had certain ambitions, however, and one day when Youngblood had killed several in a short space of time, and they were busy skinning them, about a mile away he saw a big buffalo coming almost directly toward them. Full of excitement, he implored Youngblood to let him try his luck.

"All right," was Youngblood's good-natured response. "There is the gun; go ahead!"

"I just want to kill that one," returned Allred, "so as to be able to say that I have killed a buffalo."

Youngblood nodded. Allred strapped on

the cartridge-belt, picked up the gun, and stalked off proudly with the air of a conquering hero.

The buffalo was a single one that had become separated in some way from its herd, and was coming on the full run. Allred walked quickly forward about 200 yards or so, and by this time the buffalo was close upon him. The amateur sportsman could not restrain a spasm of fright, as the huge brute, still coming toward him at a headlong pace, loomed up before him. He brought the gun to his shoulder as if about to shoot, but his alarm suddenly overpowered all other considerations, and concluding discretion to be the better part of valor, he at once turned tail and flew back to where his companions were, as if the evil one himself were behind him. At almost the same moment the buffalo perceived him, and, frightened in its turn, wheeled about and ran too. Allred never noticed this, but thinking the beast was after him, white with terror, fairly leaped over the ground, expecting at every stride to be overtaken and crushed by the hoofs of his formidable antagonist.

When he reached Youngblood and Mc-Ferrin, and found them simply holding their sides with laughter, he looked sheepish enough, especially after they had pointed out to him the buffalo rapidly disappearing in the opposite direction. But nothing could convince him, however, that he had not escaped a frightful danger, and he was effectually cured of all desire to be able to boast, on his return home, that he had killed a buffalo.

Another time, though, he was in much more genuine danger; he was out with Youngblood, and they were busily engaged in skinning the buffalo which the latter had killed, when they came to one which still showed signs of life. Youngblood concluded to whet his knife while it was dying, and to enable him to do so, laid his gun down upon the ground. He had hardly commenced the sharpening process when he was startled by a cry from Allred.

"Look out!" he screamed. "Look out!"

He turned, and to his horror saw that the animal, in one last effort, had staggered to its feet and was close upon them. There was no time to recover the gun, and they were forced to run without it. The wounded buffalo stopped at the gun, and began to paw it, at the same time digging its horns into Youngblood's coat, which had been thrown down beside it. As they had but the one gun, the two men could do nothing but retreat to a respectful distance, and calmly await developments. It was not long, however, before the beast lay down beside the gun, and soon drew its last breath, making it safe for them to return and complete their task.

CHAPTER V.

The little band finally moved from Sappy
River to Smoky River, a very small stream,
not more than a rod or two wide, and on the
banks of which grew a few straggling willows,
with here and there a lofty cotton-wood tree.
Youngblood considered this a good place to
stay for awhile and continue his hunting.
They dried the fore quarters of the buffalo
meat, and sold the hind quarters, sending
large quantities of it to Buckmaster and
Shidler, the agents in Missouri.

While at Smoky River, Youngblood
started forth one day, taking Allred with
him, in search of a herd of buffalo which,
with the aid of his field-glass, he had discovered some three miles away.

McFerrin was left behind in the camp to load cartridges.

About an hour after the departure of his companions, he happened to raise his eyes, and saw, at a short distance, a band of Indians riding down upon him. They had, doubtless, been watching the camp, and had waited for the departure of the hunters in order to plunder it at their ease.

McFerrin realized in an instant that, single-handed, he would have no chance against them, so, dodging from tree to tree, he managed to escape from the camp, and, crawling through the grass, reached the bluffs on the river and hid himself in the thick bushes, where he had a good vantage point to watch the proceedings of the marauders below.

The Indians approached with the utmost caution, and when they were within range, fired several shots into the tent. As this action elicited no response, they were satisfied that the camp was deserted, and they at once dashed in and took possession. They thoroughly rifled the camp of everything that was of any value, and then rode away to a point about a quarter of a mile distant, where they hid themselves beneath a hillside, on the road leading from Wallace to the Republican River. This was a road which was much frequented by hunters, and here they lay in ambush until their patience was rewarded by the appearance of a man driving a team and wagon. The new-comer was Charles Brown, one of a squad of hunters, who had driven ahead of the others to make ready a camp on Smoky River, leaving the rest of his company a mile or two behind, skinning some buffalo which they had killed.

In all unconsciousness the doomed man rode on, whistling and chirruping, when suddenly, from a bush just ahead of him, came a flash and a report. With a leap, he was off his wagon and started to run, but it was too late; the Indians were upon him, and before he had time to realize what had happened, another bullet laid him low—shot through the head. The red devils then began going through the contents of the wagon; but before they had succeeded in securing much plunder, they were surprised by the appearance of Brown's party over the hillside, and in a trice they were upon their horses' backs and riding rapidly away.

It took the hunters some little while to realize what had happened, but, as soon as they did, they unharnessed the horses from the wagon and started in pursuit of their friend's murderers. It was too late, however. The Indians had too good a start, and it was impossible to overtake them.

While all this was taking place, Youngblood, in blissful ignorance of it all, was about three miles away, engaged in his favorite occupation of killing buffalo. He had just finished skinning those he had shot, and, together with Allred, was in hot pursuit of one he had wounded. The ground was very uneven, and as they reached the top of a little knoll, Youngblood's quick eye caught sight of signs of life below.

"There is a herd now," he remarked to

Allred, and halted on top of the hill, ready to shoot as soon as the animals should come within range.

It was now evening and fast growing dark, but he could perceive that the moving mass was rapidly coming toward them from the right. When it was some 600 yards away he discovered, to his surprise and alarm, that instead of buffalo it was a band of mounted men, but whether whites or red-skins the gathering darkness prevented him from making sure. The cavaliers soon perceived the silhouettes of the two men as they were clearly defined against the sky. As soon as they did so, they immediately dismounted and commenced making signs, but Young-blood was determined to use every precaution, and made no reply. He was in a thorough quandary how to proceed, but concluded it best to quietly await developments. Finally, one of the men mounted his horse again and rode slowly forward toward the little knoll.

Allred was wild with excitement.

"It is an Indian," he exclaimed in a hoarse whisper. "Shoot him!"

Youngblood was very much inclined to share his companion's belief and to take his advice. He slowly raised his gun to his shoulder, but, before he could shoot, the man hailed him in a voice which he recognized as that of a white man and a friend.

When the horseman was a little closer, he called out:

"Don't shoot, Youngblood. I came near shooting you, but, thank heaven! I didn't."

It was one of the band of hunters to which Brown had belonged, and he at once proceeded to inform Youngblood of what had occurred, and asked if he would go to the spot where Brown had been killed, and put his body on the wagon so that the wolves would not get at it.

Youngblood promised to do so, and he and Allred started off at once on their homeward tramp. On the way they stumbled across an empty powder-can, which, on examination, Youngblood found to be one of his

own. This discovery filled him with the direst forebodings, for he felt confident now that the red devils had been at his camp, stolen everything he had, and, in all probability, killed McFerrin.

The two men, anxious and silent, now hurried along as fast as they could. When they were nearly home, Youngblood warned his companion to advance as cautiously as possible, as he was afraid the Indians might have left a detachment behind to lie in wait for the proprietors of the camp on their return. So they pushed carefully on until they came to the hill-side where Brown had been killed. It was very dark now, and impossible to discover anything but the wagon, so Youngblood determined to go at once to camp, and return later, when the moon would be up, to prosecute the search for the body. When they arrived at a point about 200 yards from the camp, he ordered Allred to remain quietly where he was, while he himself would push on alone and make a sort of *reconnaissance.*

5

He therefore stole ahead, making as little noise as possible and keeping both ears and eyes well open. Suddenly he perceived a figure standing on a little rise in the ground just before him. He instantly halted, with his eyes fixed upon the apparition and scarcely daring to breathe, when, to his intense relief, the man spoke, and in very low tones the welcome words reached his ear:

"Is that you, Charlie?"

He knew at once that it was McFerrin, and ran toward him, crying out to him that it was he and to have no alarm.

McFerrin, who was shivering with cold and fright, then told him of all that had happened since his departure; how the Indians had come, stolen the horses and everything they could lay their hands on, and how from his hiding-place in the bushes he had witnessed the killing of the teamster, but was utterly powerless to do anything to prevent it.

The moon soon came up, and they went down the road, where they found the poor fellow dead and frozen stiff. He was lying on his face about fifty yards from the wagon. There were six bullet-holes in his body, and the fiends had raised his scalp. It was a fearful sight, but Youngblood raised the body in his arms, threw it across his shoulder, and, carrying it to the wagon, laid it inside where it was impossible for the wolves to get at it.

This pious task accomplished, they returned in sorrowful silence to their depleted camp, where they passed a wakeful and anxious night, not daring to show much light, for fear that the red-skins might still be hovering about in the vicinity.

In the morning a squad of hunters rode up to the camp. Youngblood informed them of the raid, of which they had heard nothing, and they all then went down to the road where Brown's body lay. Loud and deep were the imprecations as they saw the murdered man, and in righteous wrath a vow of vengeance was sworn against the dastardly perpetrators of the deed.

Brown's companions, who had been chasing the Indians all night, but who had been unable to catch them, returned during the morning.

A council of war was held, and it was unanimously agreed to pursue the Indians without delay, and, if possible, mete out the fate to them that they had dealt poor Brown. The company altogether numbered twenty-six men, all armed with long-range repeating rifles, and each man was furnished with from 100 to 600 cartridges. For over seventy-five miles the trail was followed, without overtaking the foe. It was by no means easy traveling, and in many places was not unattended with danger, for the trail led constantly through deep and heavily wooded gorges and ravines, where it would have been the easiest thing in the world to have been taken in an ambush, and where everyone might have been massacred without the faintest opportunity for retaliation.

But the brave little band, bent on punish-

ing the cowardly assassins, scarcely paid
any heed to danger, but pressed steadily on,
in the hope of the sooner overtaking their
human game, until their progress was re-
tarded and finally brought to a standstill by
a furious snow-storm. The snow fell to a
depth of eight inches, and, besides prevent-
ing them from keeping on their course,
proved a serious matter in another direction,
as they were entirely dependent on grass for
fodder for their horses. The men themselves
could live well enough off the abundance of
game which they brought down with their
guns, but there was absolutely no way now
to provide for their steeds.

After considerable discussion it was agreed,
as soon as the storm abated somewhat, to
make for Fort Wallace, where there would
be no difficulty in obtaining provender, and
the chase could then be resumed. The fort
was reached without any serious mischance,
and the commander informed of the straits
in which the party found themselves. This
gentleman, however, instead of, as they

expected, at once furnishing them with sufficient feed for their horses to enable them
to continue the pursuit, decided to first send
a dispatch to General Pope, at Leavenworth,
acquainting him with the facts in the case.
The latter replied, ordering the commander
to send fifty men and four scouts to overtake
and deal summary punishment to the marauders. The four scouts selected to accompany the expedition were Hank Campbell,
Louis Allred, Bill Peach, and, to his great
satisfaction, our old friend Youngblood himself.

The trail was taken up at the point the
first band left it when they struck off for
Fort Douglas. It was not long before they
met with success. They had proceeded only a
few miles, when one of the soldiers cried out:

"See! There is a herd of buffalo over
yonder."

The captain of the company unslung his
field-glass, and, after examining the herd
carefully for a few moments, lowered the
glass, with a laugh.

"There they are, boys," he said. "If you want game, there's plenty of it. They are Indians, and well armed, too."

A halt was immediately ordered, the boxes containing cartridges were opened, and each man told to take as many as he could carry. The Captain continued to watch the enemy through his glass, and soon perceived that they had discovered the neighborhood of the soldiers, and were busily engaged in massing their forces and making other preparations for the attack. He hastily commanded his men to get into marching line—the teams were left under guard—and the company moved forward to meet the foe. The ground was smooth and level for about two miles, and the soldiers dashed on at a gallop until within about half a mile of where the Indians were drawn up, when the chief raised a flag of truce, and a moment after was seen approaching, followed by four of his men.

At a word of command from the Captain, the cavalry reined in their foaming horses and halted, to see what would be the upshot of the proceeding. When the Indians had advanced to within a few hundred yards, the Captain detailed two men to go out and meet them and inquire their business. No sooner, however, were they face to face, than the red-skins surrounded them. Suspecting treachery, the Captain immediately put spurs to his horse and galloped forward, followed by all his men.

A long talk then ensued, but with no satisfactory result, for the Indians persistently and obstinately refused to understand anything that was said to them. During the parley, one of them carelessly, and as if by accident, allowed his horse to carry him away a few paces, and rode into a ravine, where he sat with only the upper part of his face visible, intently watching every movement that took place.

As it became evident that it was hopelessly impossible to obtain anything in the slightest degree satisfactory from a parley with the chief, the Captain determined to take him and his followers prisoners. Eight men cov-

ered them with their guns, while they were forced to give up their arms. As soon as the one in the ravine saw what had taken place, he made a bolt of it, keeping himself covered by the rocks in the defile as long as he could, and then hurrying away at full gallop to the hill, behind which the band of Indians were waiting.

As the Indians were greatly superior in numbers, equally well armed, and, moreover, held much the advantage in position, the captain of the soldiers, after some little deliberation, came to the conclusion that it would be imprudent, not to say foolhardy, to attack them where they were; so he endeavored, by all sorts of artifices, to induce them to abandon their intrenched position, but the wily savages refused to be inveigled, and obstinately held their ground.

The Captain did not dare to order his men to fire upon them at random, as they had with them two German girls, whom they had abducted some time before, after murdering the rest of the family, and he knew that, at that distance, a bullet was quite as likely to strike them as an Indian. So, after some further maneuvering, which was equally fruitless, he decided, with great reluctance, that it would be best to return with the four prisoners to Fort Wallace, report the state of the case to the post commander, and leave him to deal with the situation as he should deem best.

The four Indians were, accordingly, placed under a strong guard behind the wagons, and the 'march back was begun. The cold was intense; a keen, raw, bitter wind swept over the prairie, each blast of which seemed to freeze the very marrow in the bones of the shivering soldiers. Although they had overcoats, overshoes, and mittens, more than one finger, ear, or nose was frozen before the ride was over. The power of endurance exhibited by the Indians, who were half naked, during this trying journey to the fort, struck Youngblood as little short of marvelous, and filled him with amazement. They really did not seem to suffer at all from the piercing

cold, and they, too, were under the disadvantage of being compelled to ride all the
way, while the white men could dismount
from time to time, and, by tramping about,
stir their sluggish blood into circulation
once more.

When the fort was finally reached, the
post doctor, who examined the red-skins,
declared that their exposure to the cold had
not harmed them in the slightest degree,
and this, in spite of the fact that their
feet were covered with moccasins only and
that they had very little clothing on their
bodies.

Just before the fort was reached, one of the
prisoners made a sudden dash to escape, and
would have succeeded in doing so had not a
shot brought him down. The others were
turned over to Colonel Hanbright, the commander.

Youngblood did not remain with the
troops long enough to know the ultimate fate
of the rascals, or whether any further attempt was made to punish the rest of the

band and rescue the German girls in their hands, for he happened to fall in with a man named Riley, who owned a good team of horses, and was anxious to have some shooting. Youngblood, therefore, formed a combination with him, and forthwith started out on another hunt.

CHAPTER VI.

For about four weeks Youngblood and
his new companion hunted the buffalo with
unvarying success, killing and drying during
this time over 100.

After this the game migrated and moved
about 100 miles east to the heads of several
streams, viz.: Saline, Sappy, Prairie Dog,
Beaver, and Big Timber. Our hunters followed them, and secured great numbers.

Here they chanced to meet three other
men, who joined them, increasing their number to five.

One day they took the team and sallied
forth after buffalo, leaving one of their number to guard the camp and smoke the meat.

He had wandered out a little distance to collect firewood, and hearing a noise in the camp he hurried back, supposing that his friends had returned, and wondering what could have caused them to come back in such a very short time. But, instead of the hunters, what was his horror and amazement to stumble upon fourteen red-skins, who were busily employed in appropriating everything that was within their reach. They had captured his gun, and the moment he appeared they fired upon him, but fortunately without touching him. The man, taken by surprise as he was, ran for dear life. Several of the thieves started after him and pursued him into a ravine.

He knew the direction the hunting-party had taken, and recognized that his only hope was in overtaking them. Luckily they had not gone far from camp, and as soon as the red-skins perceived them, they stopped short in the pursuit of their intended victim and beat a hasty retreat. They probably did not think it wise to return to the camp,

but joined the rest of the band on Sappy
River, where the next day, as Youngblood
graphically put it, thirty-seven of them
"died very suddenly." One of the Indians
that met this sad fate was a chief. After the
fight was over, while they were examining
the bodies, one of the white hunters discovered a sort of roll tied to this chief's side.
He unloosened it, and, holding it up in
bewilderment, asked his friends what it
could be. They examined it, and discovered,
to their horrified indignation, that it was a
dressed buckskin cape, profusely ornamented
with white women's scalps.

This is only one example out of many similar incidents, and yet there are still to be
found many people who exclaim in their
mingled sentimentality and ignorance, "Alas!
the poor Indian!" and bestow upon him any
amount of misplaced pity, which is painfully
absurd to anyone who has known intimately
the object of their solicitude.

Any old scout will tell you that his
acquaintance with our "red brother" does

not reveal in him any trait of either character
or disposition which is in any degree worthy
of respect. It is, of course, beyond question
a fact that he has been at times maltreated,
but this is no reason why we should be
blinded to what he really is—naturally lazy,
cruel, and vindictive, and a perfect type of
treachery, never acting in good faith, except
when he knows it is for his own advantage
to do so. Mercy is a virtue of which the
Indian has not the faintest conception, and
the truth is never known to fall from his lips
when a lie can be made to answer. In two
words, he can only be described as a veritable demon, who has no humane sentiment,
who will spare nothing, neither age nor sex,
who scorns all law, and whose chief delight
is to ruthlessly murder, burn, and ravage.

The little scrimmage narrated above occurred in April, 1876, and until the fall of
the same year, Youngblood and his friends
hunted peacefully without any further mo-
lestation from the red devils, who for a long
time had a salutary and terrifying remem-

brance of the white man's long-range repeating rifles.

During this summer, a band. of Ute Indians came on a hunting expedition into the neighborhood where Youngblood was, and he had an excellent opportunity of observing their manner of hunting and killing the buffalo.

The first thing they do is to select a place for a camp, if possible near some stream, so as to be within easy distance of fuel and water. The site once chosen, the squaws, who are invariably compelled to perform all the drudgery, proceed to unpack the goods and chattels, put up the tents, care for the horses, draw water, collect firewood, and, in fact, make things comfortable generally for their lords and masters, who meanwhile loll luxuriously upon the grass in some shady place, and smoke their pipes in full ease and contentment of mind and body. When the camp is all in order, one Indian is sent out to seek for a herd of buffalo, and when he has found one, he returns to camp and

6

reports his success. Then the squaws make ready the horses, the men and boys mount their ponies, and the procession is formed, the women bringing up the rear, driving the pack-horses, and furnished with knives, with which to dress the game that the men kill.

A band of Indians mounted and equipped for a buffalo-chase presents a decidedly unique and interesting appearance. Their ponies are scrawny looking little things, and many of them are so small that the feet of the rider nearly reach the ground. In spite of his size and appearance, however, the pony is by no means to be despised; there are emphatically, to use an expressive vulgarism, no flies upon him; he makes up in grit and endurance for his lack of beauty, and he will carry a rider or a heavy pack much farther in a day than an ordinary horse could possibly do. The Indian saddle is a mechanical curiosity. It is manufactured of two forked sticks, one behind and one before, held apart by two pieces of board, one on either side, and with straps of buckskin run-

ning lengthwise; the boards are placed below
the sticks, and rest upon the horse's back,
while the buckskin straps are on top, form-
ing a comfortable seat for the cavalier. Still,
although this saddle is an easy one for the
rider, it is frequently severe on the pony,
for the boards are generally very roughly
finished, and it is no unusual thing to see
the pony's back so lacerated by them that
the bone is in places perfectly bare and
exposed. This is of no consequence to the
Indian, however, for he shows no more mercy
to his horse than he does to his squaw, and
so long as he rides comfortably it is a matter
of supreme indifference to him what his pony
may be suffering, and he will even beat him
for flinching and "giving down" under the
pain inflicted by one of these instruments of
torture.

A vast deal of importance is attached to
the ceremonies which are gone through with
to propitiate Fortune and bring good luck to
the chase; and, to a person who sees them
for the first time, the performance of these

rites is almost as much of a sight as a first-class circus. As soon as they get as close to a herd as they deem it safe, they dismount and begin the performance, which consists of a vast deal of tomfoolery. When a white man has discovered his herd, he pitches right in and gets down to business at once, but nothing could induce an Indian to fire a shot until he has religiously gone through with each one of the rites suitable to the occasion, and which are his inheritance from time immemorial. He falls upon his knees and repeats long prayers, invoking the aid of the deity of the chase; then follows an exceedingly polite address to the buffalo, in which it is told that if it will be so kind as not to run away, it shall receive some tobacco, a piece of which each Indian forthwith buries in the ground; he then pulls his horse's tail, whispers in its ear, and ties eagle feathers in its tail to lend it speed. Sometimes a dog is killed, cooked, and eaten. After all this and frequently much more has been gone through with, and a certainty of good luck thereby secured, the hunters mount their ponies and speed off to the herd, which, if not frightened away by the powwow, has all this. time been quietly grazing on the prairie. As soon as the foe appears bearing down upon them, however, the buffalo take the alarm, and, in their affright, very frequently rush in a mass directly toward the hunters; but when within a short distance, they stop short, turn suddenly, and dash away with a deafening bellowing in the opposite direction.

The moment the buffalo turn is the signal for the attack, and immediately the Indians, with the wildest of yells imaginable, bear down upon them with bows and arrows, spears and guns, and the slaughter commences. Those who have guns ride to one side of the fleeing herd, and keeping parallel to them, load and fire as fast as they can, bringing down a buffalo at almost every shot; at the same time those with spears and similar weapons ride directly into the midst of the herd, and 'forcing their ponies almost against one of the animals, thrust their spears into some vital part. Those with bows and arrows also dash into the herd, and dropping the bridles, allow their ponies to follow their own heads, while they make use of both hands, shooting arrows first into one buffalo and then another. These arrows, three or four of which are shot into each animal, are generally tipped with pieces of saw-blade, on the edges of which is cut a fine beard, which causes them to work inward as the animal runs. The slaughter is often kept up until every one of the herd is slain. In the hunt which Youngblood had the good fortune to witness, 110 were killed in a space of something less than a quarter of an hour.

When the hunt is over, the squaws proceed to dress the meat and pack it upon the horses, while the men enjoy a siesta, smoking, laughing, and boasting of their various exploits. When everything is ready for departure, the men mount their ponies and ride gaily back to camp, the women following more slowly, driving the horses, which have been laden with the flesh and hides.

Though it is the custom of the Indians to use arrows with bearded tips for hunting purposes, they employ an entirely. different one when on the war-path. This latter species they poison in some way, so that they are almost certain to cause death, or, at all events, to make a very ugly sore. It is said that the method is to take a piece of meat, and by goading a rattlesnake to anger, cause it to drive its fangs into the meat, and thereby impregnate it with its venom. The meat is then left to putrefy and become thoroughly permeated with the poison, and the arrows are then plunged into the deadly mass. These poisoned arrows are kept carefully apart from those destined for hunting purposes.

The wars between the different Indian tribes are almost incessant, and more of them are killed in this way than by white men. In their wars with each other the most terrible ferocity and most relentless cruelty are exhibited, and those that are taken prisoners are invariably put to the torture.

One of Youngblood's friends, named Van Meter, once witnessed this torture of prisoners, while among the Ogallah-Sioux Indians, and his description of it is most appalling.

The Ogallahs were on the war-path, and one day, in a slight skirmish with the Crows, they succeeded in taking one of the latter captive, a warrior about twenty years of age. Preparations were at once made for the administration of the torture. The young Crow was first stripped and bound to a wagon-wheel, while a large pine plank was shaved into small splinters. An Ogallah warrior was then selected as executioner, and the rest prepared to perform the war-dance about their victim. The one chosen to apply the torture took a knife, and taking up a piece of the prisoner's flesh between his thumb and finger, cut a deep gash in it, and thrust into the wound thus made a bunch of pine splinters, which he then set on fire and allowed to burn out. As soon as one set of splinters had died out, another was

inserted as before, but in a fresh gash. This was continued until the miserable youth's skin was burned to a crisp all over his body. Notwithstanding the intolerable agony he must have suffered, he never uttered a cry, nor exhibited any signs of pain, but, to all intents and purposes, appeared more unconcerned than most people would in simply witnessing such torture. While this was going on, the Ogallahs kept up an incessant weird and unearthly dance, circling round and round about their victim with fiendish yells and cries, and every now and then making as if to strike him with their spears and tomahawks. When his flesh was completely charred, and he was almost dead, he was tomahawked and scalped. Horrible as this whole description sounds, the proceeding is of very frequent occurrence among the Indians. In this respect they are apt to be more cruel toward each other than toward the whites, although more than one innocent white man has suffered terrible torture at their cruel hands.

CHAPTER VII.

Youngblood's next camping-place was
Silver Lake, situated in a large canebrake
near the head of Pawnee River, between that
stream and "White Woman" Creek. He
was absolutely forced from his former hunting-grounds, because the Indians had chased
all the buffalo away. It is no uncommon
thing for them to drive them, on horseback,
as far as 200 miles.

"White Woman" Creek, his new stamping-ground, was named by the Indians, and,
as usual with Indian nomenclature, had a
real reason for its title. Some years previous, a woman named Harn was captured
by the Indians, and taken away prisoner.
During the course of their journey they

camped for a night on the banks of this
creek, but before they left the next morning they outraged the poor woman, drove a
stake through her body, and left her there;
hence the name of the stream. It is sometimes called "Suffering Woman;" and in an
account of a fight which Colonel Lewis had
with the Indians on this creek, in which
Lewis and five of his men were killed, it is
called "Spanish Woman," but among all
frontiersmen it is known as "White
Woman."

Between Pawnee River and "White
Woman" Creek was a long extent of very
flat, low country, full of large lakes and
dense canebrakes. In his camp at Silver
Lake, Youngblood was entirely alone. He
had brought no one with him, and his only
company in the midst of the big, dreary
swamp, were buffalo and antelope by day,
and at night wolves, who evinced a much
stronger predilection for the hunter's society
than he did for theirs. The wolves had been
in the habit of subsisting chiefly upon the

carcasses of the buffalo left by the hunters,
who had killed them for their hides; and as
it was now late in October, and no hunters
had been in the locality for some time, the
wolves had become fierce and ravenous, and
were ready to attack anything—horses, and
even men.

One day Youngblood had been out hunting, and had succeeded, after a long day's
tramp, in killing one buffalo late in the afternoon. As it was rapidly growing dark, and
as there was danger of his losing his way if
he attempted to find his camp, he determined
to remain where he was for the night. He
moved his wagon close to where the buffalo
lay, made his bed upon the ground, and
spread the hide of the buffalo over him, with
the wooly side down. He had hardly closed
his eyes, however, before the wolves, attracted by the scent of the freshly killed
meat, began gathering from all the neighboring thickets. They soon devoured the buffalo, with low growlings and sharp cracklings
of their teeth, which were anything but

pleasant sounds to the recumbent hunter, who began to think that they might make their dessert off of him. His gun was in the wagon, and he did not dare to rise and make the attempt to possess himself of it. Some of the wolves became so bold that they ventured close to where he lay, and began to pull and tug at the hide which served him as a quilt. This was decidedly alarming, but by singing and shouting he managed to frighten them away, until, gorged by their meal, they decided to leave him in peace.

Youngblood remained at Silver Lake for about a month, meeting with very fair success as regards the amount of game killed, but finding it very difficult to obtain a market for the meat. After being alone all this time, he fell in with a man named Fred Armstrong, who declared that he was a "regular world-beater" at killing buffalo and deer, and urged his new acquaintance to go back with him into the mountains, which he said were teeming with black-tailed deer. Youngblood finally allowed himself to be persuaded, although this necessitated a journey of over 200 miles. Their way lay through a barren sort of country where game was very scarce, and their stock of provisions, of which they had taken only a scanty supply, got so low that the question of subsistence soon became a very serious one. Although there was no game, there was plenty of cattle about belonging to the different ranches; and finally, in despair, Armstrong declared that he was going to shoot a calf, and selected a yearling which had become separated from the herd. Before he could raise his gun, however, three cow-boys suddenly appeared around a little hillock.

"Good Lord!" whispered Armstrong, "I'm glad I didn't shoot, for they would have been onto us before the calf had quit kicking."

Luckily for him, however, the cow-boys did not guess his intentions, but rode along with the two hunters to a spring, near which they said there were plenty of deer to be found.

Here they camped for the night, and the

next morning, early, before his companion
was up, Youngblood started forth with his
gun to try his luck.

He had not gone more than a quarter of a
mile before he saw that the cow-boys had
spoken the truth; there were plenty of tracks,
and he at once began to keep a sharp lookout for deer.

Stealing cautiously up a hill, he peered
over the top, and, to his immense satisfaction
and delight, saw four deer walking single
file along a cow-path.   He aimed at the foremost one, which was a fine doe, and at the
crack of his gun she sank to the ground, and
the second and third followed in quick suc-
cession, each brought down by a single shot.
The fourth was a lordly buck, which came
running up the bluff to the spot where the
hunter was; but the latter was ready for him,
and once more " old poison-slinger " got in
its work.

As it was impossible for him to transport
the booty himself, Youngblood returned to
the camp, where Armstrong still lay in the

arms of Morpheus. He did not awaken him,
but, taking a horse, went back to where the
deer were and loaded three of them on its
back.

On his way back he met Armstrong, who
rubbed his eyes in amazement, saying:
"Hello! If that's your way of doing things,
I guess I'll have to go back on what I said
about being a world-beater." But when he
heard that there was a big buck besides, he
began to think that Youngblood knew something about hunting, too, and he acknowl-
edged that he had been gotten ahead of in
great shape, and he would have to yield his
title to his companion.

The two men remained together for something over two months, and as during that
time Youngblood averaged about six deer
to Armstrong's one, he ceased to take any
stock in the latter's claim to be a " world-
beater." The opinion of each as to the
other's prowess received a rather amusing
illustration during the stay of a visitor they
happened to have at the camp. This visitor,

7

in the course of conversation with Armstrong, happened to ask him what sort of a
hunter Youngblood was. Armstrong's reply
was that he was a poor shot, but the luckiest
killer he ever saw in his life. A short time
afterward he went to Youngblood and asked
his opinion of Armstrong. "Well," was
the response, "he is a first-rate hunter, but
about the worst killer that I was ever acquainted with." At this the visitor laughed
heartily, in which merriment he was joined
by the other two, as soon as its cause was
explained.

But it was not long before Youngblood
found that, in addition to the deer, there
were, in the mountains, other and much
more formidable animals, panthers and
mountain lions, which, in fact, are almost
always to be met with in places frequented
by deer, on which they chiefly subsist. Their
plan of stalking their game is to climb a tree
which has a limb extending over some path
used by the deer, or to conceal themselves
behind something near this path, and then,

when the deer passes under or near them, they spring upon and kill it. The blood they are particularly fond of, and they commonly tear open the throats of the victims, and eagerly lap up the fluid as it flows warm from the veins. They eat the flesh also, and are so strong that they can carry away a full-sized deer.

Youngblood one day fired at and wounded a deer; but as he was pursuing it, he came upon a large drove, so he concluded to leave the wounded one and come back and seek for it later. This, however, he was unable to do until the next morning, and taking up the trail where he had left it the previous day, he had only followed it for a short distance when he came to a place where he perceived unmistakable evidences of a desperate struggle. After a careful examination, he came to the conclusion that the wounded deer had been attacked and carried off by some animal or other. Curious to know more about it, he continued to follow the trail, which was by no means a difficult thing to do, as the hair of the deer had been rubbed off against the stones and twigs, and everywhere there were fresh traces of blood. When he had proceeded about half a mile, he stumbled upon the entrails of the deer lying upon the ground. To his astonish-ment, these entrails were not torn to pieces, but, on the contrary, were entire, as if some skillful hunter had cut them out with his knife. He then began to look cautiously around to discover the cause of this phenom-enon, when suddenly, just in front of him, about twenty paces off, a mountain lion darted into view, and, before he had time to aim, disappeared into a neighboring thicket. He fired, however, but apparently without hitting it, for there was no result but a loud roar, and the crunching of the branches as a heavy body passed through them. He waited for some time, hoping that the lion would return; but in this he was disap-pointed, for the beast, gorged with its prey, had probably gone off into the thicket for an after-dinner snooze.

Even more numerous and dangerous than the mountain lions are the panthers, and when there was fresh meat in the camp they would yell frightfully all night long. To anyone not used to it, their screams have a horrible sound, and are a most effectual sleep-dispeller; but once accustomed to it, Youngblood found that he paid no more attention to them than he would to the hoots of the night-owl in Indiana.

Until the snow began to melt, and the deer to disappear, as they always do when the snow has gone, our two hunters remained in the mountains. As Youngblood did not care to follow the migration of the game, he concluded to go back to the plains, and try his luck once more at buffalo.

CHAPTER VIII.

BACK TO KANSAS—AT ODDS—THE BITER BIT —EMIGRANTS ON A HUNT—INDIANS, NOT BUFFALO.

After the deer left the mountains, Young-blood went back to Kansas, about 200 miles east on the Arkansas River, to a point not far from the head of Pawnee River, in Buffalo County. With the skill he had acquired, he could now kill all the buffalo he wanted to, so he needed no assistance in that way; but the trouble had been to find a means to get the meat to market. He therefore hired three men, none of whom were hunters, to transport the fruits of his rifle.

They took up their quarters on Alkali Lake, and all went well for a time. But it was not long before Youngblood discovered that his three men were not destined to live in amity together; in fact, there were only

too unmistakable signs that there was bad
blood between them. For some reason or
other, two of them evidently bore a strong
grudge against the other, and were continu-
ally imposing upon him, losing no opportunity to taunt and insult him. Things
began to look pretty threatening, when a certain incident, at all events, prevented the
shedding of blood, for the one so annoyed
had frequently threatened to kill the other
two, and had even asked Youngblood to
lend him his gun, having already provided
himself with cartridges.

All four were out one day, when they
struck a large herd of buffalo. Foreseeing
that he was likely to have severe work
ahead of him, and that his pocket-book might
get lost, Youngblood handed it to the teamster to keep for him until the hunt should be
over. The man and the pocket-book he
never saw again, for no sooner was he out of
his sight than the teamster jumped into the
wagon and drove off. When Youngblood
returned to camp that night, and found

the man missing, he saw at once what it all meant, and consulted with the other men. They asked to be allowed to take another team and wagon, and to go in pursuit of the fugitive. To this their master finally consented, and drove them to the nearest railway station. They formed a correct guess as to the direction the thief was likely to take, headed him off, and finally captured him and took him to Las Animas, in Colorado. Here they brought him before a justice of the peace, and, with supreme effrontery, one of them swore that the team, which really belonged to the runaway, was his, and proved it by the affidavit of the other. The magistrate remanded the prisoner to jail, and turned over the horses and wagon, together with the pocket-book, to his captors. These latter returned his own property to Youngblood, but kept the team for themselves, while they left the thief to languish in jail until his case was called, when he was discharged, as there was no one to appear against him.

Soon after this incident, Youngblood went to Sherlock with a load of meat. Here he found a large number of emigrants, most of whom were provided with good teams, and some he found anxious to go out on a hunt. He proposed to give them half the meat if they would haul it in to market, and he experienced no difficulty in finding several persons who were willing to accept this offer. So he started out with three teams, ten men, and three women, all inspired with the eager desire to see something of a sort of life far different from anything to which they had been accustomed. After proceeding for about twenty-five miles, they found a place to camp for the night, and while the men were making the necessary preparations and the women busied themselves in getting supper, Youngblood sallied forth and shot a buffalo. The whole company went into ecstasies over the tenderloins, which were soon fried and ready for distribution.

The next morning they moved on, as the women complained of the alkali water.

When they reached a good spring, about ten miles off, they found, camped near it, a band of Indians, who, however, fled on the approach of the white men, and so hastily that they left their meat roasting before the fire. In spite of this, however, the emigrants were so frightened that they could not be persuaded to remain long enough to get a drink, but, wheeling their wagons around, they started for Sherlock at a sweeping trot, looking around every few minutes, as if they expected to see an army of painted demons thirsting for their blood and hankering for scalps. Youngblood was so disgusted with them that he made little effort to turn them from their determination or pacify their silly fright, but let them continue on their retreat to Sherlock, which they reached in safety, without the slightest injury to any of them.

Youngblood did not remain long in the town, but, in company with another man, went off to his old hunting-ground, the source of the Pawnee River. While here, they were driving one day along the bank of the river, where the bluffs rose beside them to a considerable height, when, on looking over, our hunter saw something which he took for a herd of buffalo that had come down to the water to drink. He jumped from the wagon, and ran down the bluffs to where he could see the tops of their humps. As he was going at full speed, he suddenly ran into a gang of squaws, who were guarding a lot of horses. He then recognized that what he had taken for buffalo were Indians, crawling up the small ridge which overlooked the spot where he was. He saw that he was in a close place, and, not stopping to ask any questions, he hurried back to the wagon and informed his companion of what he had discovered. The latter was in a terrible fright, and asked tremblingly if there was any danger of the red-skins coming after them. Youngblood, who had had too many experiences of this kind to feel very anxious, replied coolly:

" Well, if they do, we can kill as many of them as they do of us."

This seemed but poor consolation to the other, however, who did not see how that would be any comfort to a dead man.

While still discussing the Indians, a herd of buffalo came in sight. They killed four, and, loading the meat upon the wagon, drove to Pierceville, the nearest station, where they found a company of soldiers, who had come in search of the Indians they had seen.

CHAPTER IX.

THE SOLDIERS' LAGGING CHASE OF INDIANS
—ALL DRESS-PARADE AND NO SENSE—A
GREENY CATCHES A BUFFALO CALF—"HELP
ME TO LET IT GO."

The soldiers, commanded by a Captain
Payne, were under orders to overhaul a
band of eighty Indians who were reported to
have crossed the Kansas Pacific Railroad,
near Monument Station, and who were evidently bent on mischief. As soon as the Captain heard that a hunter had arrived in town
from the plains, he sent for Youngblood,
and the following colloquy took place:

"Have you seen any Indians?"

"Yes, a large band."

"When?"

"This morning."

"Where were they?"

"Near the head of Pawnee River."

"Will you go with us and help us find them?"

Youngblood laughed.

"What do you want to find them for?" he asked. "Are you going to take them some blankets?"

"No, by G--d," was the emphatic response, "I am not. We have some pills for them, and if you are a good hand to see that the medicine is properly administered, you can have a chance. Can you go?"

Youngblood considered a moment.

"Well," he said at last, "there is nothing to prevent my doing so that I know of, but I am getting tired of chasing Indians under officers who won't let us hurt them after we've caught them."

"Just give me a trial."

"Well, if you will promise to take no prisoners and not let one of them escape, I'll go; but if there's going to be any fooling about it, you can count me out."

"All right," said the Captain, laughing. "Come along!"

Orders to mount were at once given, the start was soon made, and within four hours they reached the place where Youngblood had seen the Indians. They had departed, but evidently only a short time before, as their camp-fires were still burning. The trail showed that they had gone down the bed of the Pawnee River. It still wanted two hours to sunset, and it would have been easy to have made ten or twelve miles more before darkness set in; but, to Youngblood's infinite disgust, the Captain, after surveying the ground, said: " Well, we might as well camp here for the night," which was equivalent to saying: "We will give them all the chance we can to get away."

It was fully 10 o'clock the next morning before the Captain was ready to start, and even then he brought his men out on dress-parade, as if they were some militia regiment camping out for the fun of the thing. His command consisted of two companies, who had been piloted from Fort Wallace by an old buffalo-hunter named Sam Shrike, a

8

good man, and one who would have been both able and willing to have done his part, if the Captain had shown more sense and energy. There were also a train of four six-horse teams, an ambulance, and a surgeon. The latter called forth a grim smile from our hero, as he did not see any chance of his services being called into requisition, unless one of the men should meet with some accident on dress-parade.

A fresh start was finally made, however, and after marching down the river bank a few miles it became necessary to cross to the other side, which caused further delay, more than four hours being wasted in cutting down the banks so that the wagons could be taken over. But a short distance after crossing the river they came to a spot which the Captain thought would make a good place to camp, so he ordered a halt, and said, as they might not find another location so suitable to their purpose, they would lay off there for the rest of the day. The next morning there was another dress-parade, and the sun was high in the heavens before the line of march was resumed.   They went about twenty miles down the river, and crossed back at the mouth of a stream called Buckner Creek, where they struck a beaver dam, where the water was about eight feet deep.   Here one of the soldiers dismounted, threw out a fish-line, and soon caught a fine lot of fish, which was the occasion of great excitement, as it promised a good supper.   The horses were turned loose, and the troop rested until noon the next day, when, after the customary dress-parade, the Captain directed his course toward Fort Dodge, which was reached in safety without the loss of a man, and with no reason to call upon the services of either surgeon or ambulance.   Here, after four days' aimless journeying, Youngblood received his discharge, and returned to Pierceville.   This Indian chase is a fair sample of the manner in which government troops are in the habit of hunting red-skins.   One old hunter is, every time, worth more than a dozen soldiers.

On his return to Pierceville, Youngblood found that one of his horses had been bitten by a snake and was of no further use, but he managed to find among the emigrants a man who owned a good team and who was willing to go with him. This man was about fifty years old, and had never seen a buffalo, so everything was new to him, and all that he saw filled him with wonder. The first night they camped near the head of the Pawnee River, and the next morning started north to what is known as Hackberry Creek. As they were driving along, toward sundown, Youngblood's companion, who was the taller of the two, suddenly cried out: "Laws! Look there." Youngblood rose in the wagon, and was not a little surprised to see, just on the other side of a long, low ridge, and within easy gun-shot, a herd of about 2,000 buffalo. They were grazing quietly, and had not perceived the approach of the hunters. Taking his gun, Youngblood slipped to the top of the ridge and fired several times, killing two. After dressing one, he went to the other, which was a cow, and was lying about a hundred yards from the first. Her calf had lain down beside her, and Youngblood told his man to slip behind the cow and catch it. "All right," said he; "and when I have gripped it, you must come and help me." With this he got down on his hands and knees and crawled up close to the dead cow; but the calf caught sight of him, and getting up, walked round the cow to meet him. As the calf appeared, he lay as flat on the ground as he could, expecting to catch it as soon as it came within reach; but, to his surprise and consternation, when within about eight feet of him it suddenly sprang upon him and began trampling and goring him in a most lively manner. The calf was not old enough to do him much harm, so Youngblood, who was splitting his sides with laughter, did not interfere, but allowed them to fight it out by themselves. The man, who was frightened almost out of his wits, struggled and yelled for help, and finally managed to get on his feet, and ran for dear life. The calf followed him about a dozen feet, and then turned quietly back and lay down again by the cow. As soon as Youngblood could restrain his laughter, he took the case in hand, and the calf was soon secured.

The next morning bright and early they started on the trail of the herd, and about 10 o'clock they came in sight of them traveling westward toward Silver Lake, which was about twenty miles distant. Until about 2 o'clock in the afternoon they followed them with the wagon, but without succeeding in overtaking them. The other man was in despair, but Youngblood told him that he would soon manage it, and forthwith proceeded to mount a good saddle-horse they had with them. Then, telling his companion to follow slowly so as not to frighten the buffalo, he galloped off to one side of the herd, and riding through a deep draw, got ahead of them; picketing his horse, he now lay down almost in their course and waited. Not until they were within thirty yards did he open fire, but when he did it was with good effect, and by the time his partner came up he had killed ten. When dressed, this made a good load, and the hunters started for Pierceville, and, after traveling all night, arrived there about daylight. The town was full of emigrants, and there was no trouble in disposing of the meat at good prices.

CHAPTER X.

MEANNESS WHICH DID NOT PAY—TOO CON-
FIDENT HUNTERS — DANGERS OF THE
PLAINS—BACK TO MISSOURI ONCE MORE.

Some of the emigrants, however, refused
to buy, saying that it was cheaper and easier
to go out and kill their own meat. The old
hunter laughed in his sleeve as he saw them
cleaning up their guns preparatory to a
grand slaughter of the unfortunate buffalo,
and he remarked that he was afraid his occupation would be gone, as it appeared as if
they were going to kill off all the game.
The emigrants did not relish his joking much,
and told him just to wait until they returned.

"All right," said Youngblood, good-
naturedly; "but be sure and take plenty
of teams to bring in the meat. It would be
a pity to have to leave it to rot on the plains
for lack of transportation."

Shortly after their departure, Youngblood

left Pierceville, alone, and went to Alkali
Lake, fifteen miles from the head of the
Pawnee River. While driving along Dry
Lake he saw a squad of men about a mile
off in the basin of the lake. They perceived
him at the same time, and commenced making signals of distress, running toward him,
waving their hats, and calling on him to stop.
As soon as they were near enough he recognized his old friends, the emigrants, who had
started out so full of confidence from Pierceville. The poor fellows were in a sad plight,
as they were almost dying from thirst, not
having seen a drop of water for three days.
Several of their horses had given out, and
they had been digging with their knives, hoping to strike water in the basin of Dry Lake.
Youngblood could not help pitying them,
although they had been mean enough to run
the chance of losing their lives on the unknown plains rather than pay him a few
dollars, and he took them to a spring at the
foot of a hill about a quarter of a mile away,
where they could obtain all the pure, fresh

water they wanted. They were half-starved as well, and if Youngblood had not happened along, would probably have perished. Men who are unacquainted with the plains have no business upon them unaccompanied by a pilot. There is no lack of water, for there are plenty of springs that never go dry; but to one who is not acquainted with their location it is a difficult matter to find them, and a person may suffer horribly from thirst, and perhaps even die within a few steps of water. Another reason why a pilot is indispensable is that the novice, not knowing how to hunt or where to look for game, might wander for weeks and never see a buffalo, or if he should stumble upon a herd, the chances are that if left to himself he would not be able to kill a single one. Then, most emigrants, and people who come from the East to hunt on the plains, are armed with squirrel rifles and shot-guns, which are of no possible use in hunting big game. Therefore, for one's own convenience and safety, even, it is the wisest thing to do to

hire a pilot, even if his pay is $5 a day.
Shortly after this, Youngblood concluded
to return to Missouri and spend a few weeks
with his family. He reached home the 13th
of June, 1876, and remained there until
October, when he grew weary of civilization,
and longed for the free, untrammeled life of
the plains once more; so, taking with him
his oldest son and a man named Baker, he set
out in quest of further adventures in the
Great West.

CHAPTER XI.

He decided to make at once for his old
haunt on the Pawnee River; but the rivers
all through Kansas were badly swollen, and
in places it was almost impossible to make
any headway, so it was full fourteen days
before his destination was reached. He concluded to take up his headquarters at Clear
Lake. When within a few miles of the lake,
as he was driving leisurely along with his
son and Baker, he spied a solitary buffalo
grazing not far off; but before they could
come within range the animal perceived them,
and was off in a twinkling. Youngblood, fortunately, happened to have a pony along with
him, which he had captured in a skirmish
with the Cheyennes, and he mounted it and

started in pursuit. The pony had been trained to the business, and crowded the buffalo so close that it turned and showed fight; but before he could do any damage, a shot brought him low, and when the wagon came up Youngblood had nearly finished dressing him. This was the first buffalo the other two had ever seen, and they were greatly delighted. They camped that night at Alkali Lake, and had a plentiful supper of buffalo-meat, which Baker and Youngblood's son thought was the finest thing they had ever eaten. The old hunter smiled at their enthusiasm, and, it being no novelty to him, did not care to taste it, for it was as old as he was, and as poor as a snake. The next morning was dreary and stormy, but they hitched up the horses and drove about five miles, when they ran into a squad of hunters. Game appeared to be very plentiful, and the fusillade was continuous. Our friends continued their way to the foot of the "White Woman," but, as water was scarce there, they soon drifted back into the lake region.

One evening, when the little company had halted near Silver Lake and camped on a small branch for the night, Baker, who had strolled away a short distance from the camp, suddenly called out:

"Oh, look over there! What a gang of badgers."

Youngblood ran to find out what he meant, and he saw that his gang of badgers was really a herd of buffalo, with the tips of their humps just visible above the crest of a little hillock. He hurried back, seized his gun, and stealing to the top of the ridge, succeeded in killing twelve. These, when dressed, made so good a load that they carted them at once to Sherlock, and shipped them to market. After this was accomplished, they returned and took up their abode on Alkali Lake. Leaving Baker to make a dugout—a hut dug in the bank of a branch or the brink of a hill—Youngblood, with his son Jimmie, went out about four miles, where they found the carcass of a buffalo, preyed on by a number of wolves. As wolf-skins brought excellent prices in the market, Youngblood concluded he would put some strychnine in the carcass, camp near by, and await the result; and he was well paid for his trouble, for when he went back the next morning to observe the effects of the poison, he found the dead bodies of thirteen wolves. These, with the assistance of his son, he skinned, and laden with the pelts he started back to the wagon. They had gone but a short distance, however, before they struck a large herd of buffalo, coming toward them on the run. The hunter, leaving Jimmie in charge of the skins, threw himself down in the grass and awaited the coming of the herd until they were within about twenty yards of him, when he opened fire; but out of twenty shots he succeeded in killing only six. Meanwhile, poor Jimmie was greatly alarmed, for he could not see his father, and imagined he was being trampled upon by the heavy hoofs, until he heard the firing and was undeceived. Scarcely had the herd passed when Jimmie perceived a horseman

RANDMᶜNALLY·OC

coming toward them, and called his father's attention to it. After a little scrutiny the latter saw that it was an Indian, and told Jimmie so. At this the boy fell into a terrible state of alarm, cried, and wished he had not come; but when several more appeared in sight, it was as much as his father could do to pacify him. As they came close, Youngblood raised his gun to his shoulder, and ordering the foremost of them to halt, asked him what tribe they belonged to.

"Omaha," was the reply.

"How many of you are there?"

"Thirty."

This was about correct, as Youngblood could see for himself. The Indian then inquired as to the number of the white man's party. The Indians were directly in the road to the camp, and did not look particularly friendly, but Youngblood answered boldly that they were eight, and advised the Indians to turn to the left, as some of the boys might want to shoot if they saw them. This he did, carefully watching for "the boys," but

9

not meeting with any success. This little ruse having succeeded, our hero and his trembling son made a bee-line for home. The Indians pitched their tepees upon a hill about a mile from the camp, and it was evident that they intended to remain there for the night. As it was much earlier in the day than they would ordinarily begin to make preparations for the night, and as the site they had selected was not very accessible to water, Youngblood's suspicions became aroused, and he at once began to put things in the best order for defense, in case his little camp should be attacked. It looked very much as if the red-skins had taken up their position in order to watch the hunters, and possibly attack them before daybreak. As a precaution, Youngblood picketed a horse on a knoll, about a hundred yards from camp, so that if they came he would be warned before they were absolutely upon him. A horse is about the best possible guard against a surprise by Indians, being much superior in that respect to a dog. The latter is apt to make altogether too much noise, and so give the alarm to the Indians as well, while the horse only snorts at most, and, moreover, does not sleep as much or as soundly as the dog, and seldom allows himself to be surprised. If Indians are approaching, no matter how craftily, he is sure to discover it and let his master know of it by his restlessness, sniffing, and snorting.

The fears of the hunter, however, proved groundless on this occasion, for the red-skins gave no sign. The horse exhibited no symptoms of alarm, but Youngblood continued to watch him until about 9 o'clock the next day.

The morning was very foggy, and it was not until 10 o'clock that the atmosphere cleared sufficiently to render it safe to make a reconnoiter. As soon as he considered it feasible, Youngblood took his gun and ammunition, and in company with his son proceeded to the hill where the Indians had pitched their camp the day before. There was no sign of them now, excepting the ashes of their deserted fires, and after a close

examination to discover which way they had
gone, their trail was found leading toward
White Woman Creek.

Some time afterward Youngblood learned
that, while on their march, they came very
near capturing another hunter. This man
lived in a dug-out, and was preparing his supper, when he saw the savages bearing down
upon him. One man against thirty in an
open fight was without a chance, so he rushed
into his dug-out, slammed the door to and
made it fast. The Indians soon came up and
tried to burst in. The door was not of the
strongest, and as the man inside thought
that he was doomed to death anyhow, he
determined to sell his life as dearly as possible, and began to shoot through the door at
his would-be slayers.

A great many of the Indians were wounded
by his bullets, and they soon abandoned the
plan of breaking down the door as a bad and
costly job, and turned their attention to the
top of the dug-out. But they were even less
successful there, for the interior of the hut

was dark, and the hunter, aiming through the smoke-hole, could bring them down with his gun, while affording no target himself. They soon got tired of this, and retreated, leaving the man unharmed. Indians will never fight unless they are pretty confident they can do so without injury to any one of their number.

An old Ogallah chief once declared in Youngblood's hearing, that it did not pay to give man for man, and that he would not do it. One resolute and experienced white man can hold fifty Indians at bay, if he has a good position and understands how to derive the most advantage from it.

As we related above, the red-skins, finding that they could not get at the man in the dug-out without considerable loss to themselves, retreated and took up their station on a little hill a short distance away. As soon as it was dark, the hunter crept out, and, although running a great risk, he managed to elude his bloodthirsty enemies and effect his escape. But, although thus lucky this

time, the poor fellow was soon after overtaken by a worse fate, if any fate can be
worse than that of falling into the hands of
the red devils.

He and his two partners were out hunting,
when they were caught in a heavy snow-
storm, frozen to death, and their bodies half-
devoured by wolves before they were discovered.

Youngblood himself had a narrow escape
from a similar frightful experience. He and
his son were out hunting, and had been in
pursuit of two buffalo calves for about twelve
miles before they finally captured them at a
point about six miles from Silver Lake.
They were on their way to the lake, when
the weather suddenly began to turn piercing
cold, and there was every sign of an
approaching blizzard. They hurried on at
as rapid a pace as possible, and when within
about a mile of the lake and shelter, they saw
away to their left an unusually large herd of
buffalo, fully 2,000 of them. All Youngblood's hunting instincts were aroused, and

he could scarcely conquer his desire to take advantage of such a magnificent opportunity, but the sun was almost down and the cold was increasing, so he decided it would be the only wise policy to go to the spring and wait till morning before trying his luck. As they lay down for the night, he noticed a very black cloud overhanging the horizon, and the next morning, alas for his hopes of game, the snow was a foot deep and still falling, and the air was bitterly cold. He called out to his son to lie still until the storm should abate, but the boy soon grew weary of this, and got up to kindle a fire. This, however, he could not succeed in doing, and he was soon crying so bitterly with the cold that his father arose, and after several futile attempts finally managed to obtain a blaze. The horses had strayed off in search of shelter, and were nowhere to be found, and Sherlock was thirteen miles away. It seemed little short of madness to try to wade there through the drifting snow, but Jimmie begged so piteously that his father finally consented to make the attempt; but after starting he more than once regretted it, for the cold was even more piercing and the traveling more difficult than he had anticipated. The snow was whirling all about them in huge drifts, and the fierce wind blew the frozen particles into their clothes until they became so stiff that walking knee-deep through the snow was terribly fatiguing. Their progress was necessarily very slow, and it was several hours before they reached a house and could obtain the longed-for food, shelter, and warmth. After they had eaten something, Youngblood was still shivering, and at the suggestion of the woman of the house seated himself close to a red-hot stove, pressing his legs almost against the glowing mass of coals.

He had not been seated there long, however, before he suddenly discovered that there was something wrong with his feet. At first they had felt only numb, but they now began to ache and throb, and in a short time the pain became so intense that it was almost unbearable.

He went to bed with his socks on, but his suffering was so keen as to dispel all idea of sleep, and the next morning he discovered, to his horror, that his feet were almost perfectly black, frightfully swollen, and covered with blisters.

There was no longer any doubt about it, his feet were badly frozen; and the unlucky application of heat had been about the worst thing that could possibly have been done. A very serious matter it proved to our poor hunter, for at the end of twenty days there were symptoms of mortification, and he was put on a train and taken to Fort Dodge, a distance of sixty miles, for medical treatment. Here a physician was employed, who burned off the dead flesh and scraped the bone, and at the end of seven months the patient was able to walk a little; but it was a much longer time before he entirely recovered from his lameness.

CHAPTER XII.

As soon as he was sufficiently recovered, Youngblood, with his son, returned to Sherlock, and again started in hunting. He could walk only with great difficulty, and he was forced to drive in a wagon as near a herd as he could, and then crawl on his hands and knees to within range.

From Sherlock he went west about twenty miles, and then, crossing the Arkansas River, went about thirty miles, to Cimarron Creek. After following this stream about ten miles, he struck a large herd of buffalo, and in spite of his infirmity succeeded in killing three.

After this they went about ten miles farther along the road, and camped for the

night.   Early the next morning, Jimmie
Youngblood, who had gone out to attend to
the horses, warned his father that there were
buffalo close by.   One was soon brought
down, and the others gathered, bellowing,
about the carcass.   To shoot them thus was
child's play to the experienced hunter, and
he fired at his ease until he had killed nine.
Only five miles were made that day, when
they again stopped for the night.   The next
morning, to their dismay, they found that
one of their horses was dead; but Youngblood sent his son after a team.   One of his
old partners, fortunately, happened to be in
town, and, only too glad to help his friend
out of a scrape, came and hauled the meat
for him.

There was no difficulty in obtaining another
horse, and Youngblood was soon again on
the track of the buffalo, this time about forty
miles back on Cimarron Creek.   The first
night he camped in the bed of a dry lake
and slept in the wagon.   When he raised his
head in the morning and peeped out, he saw

something about two miles away that looked like a herd of buffalo, but he was not quite sure, and rousing his son, he asked him to see if his younger eyes could make out what it was. The boy, half-awake, turned to look in the opposite direction, and there, bearing straight toward them, and almost upon them, was a herd fully a mile long and a quarter of a mile wide. With a yell, he called his father's attention to the great sight. Youngblood hurried to get his gun, but by the time he was ready the buffalo were within twenty paces of him. As they went thundering past, making the rocks and trees resound with their trampling and bellowing, he put in good work, and by the time they had passed he had a fine load, which, after dressing, he took back to market.

Jimmie now left him and went back to Missouri, so he hired in his place a man named George Daniels, to whom he gave $30 a month. This proved an unprofitable investment, however, for Daniels only stayed about three weeks, when the Indians scared

him away.   He had been sent out one morning after the horses, and when about a
quarter of a mile from camp, he discovered a
couple of Indians riding toward him.   Leaving the horses to take care of themselves, he
came flying into camp, screaming and yelling for help at every stride.   His cries
brought his master out to see what was the
matter, and, sure enough, the red-skins were
close upon the poor wretch.   The sight of
the hunter and his rifle persuaded them to
stop, however, and they at once turned tail
and rode away.   This adventure was altogether too much for Daniels' nerves, and he
declared that he wouldn't stay for $500 a
month.   .

"Nonsense," laughed Youngblood. "Such
little brushes are nothing when one gets used
to them."

"But I should never get used to them,"
replied the other, with a shudder. "Why,
there's everything that's horrible out here—
snakes, skunks, centipedes, tarantulas, and
Indians."

Youngblood tried to reassure him by telling him that if he wasn't born to be killed by an Indian he wouldn't be, and if he was, he couldn't escape it anyhow.

"Born or not born," was the skeptical answer, "they would have had me if it hadn't been for you."

" But unless it was God's will, He would not allow them to hurt you."

"I would rather depend upon you than God when the Indians are after me," answered the incorrigible Daniels.

There was no satisfaction to be gotten out of him, and there was no use in arguing with him. The man's cowardice made his life a misery to him; there was scarcely anything that he was not afraid of. One day he borrowed Youngblood's gun to shoot an antelope with. He was stealing slyly up to the animal, when, to Youngblood's amazement, he suddenly turned and came running toward the wagon at full speed.

" What in the world is the matter ?" cried Youngblood. "Why," he exclaimed, "didn't you see the lightning? I don't want any steel in my hands when there's lightning round. Why, I've jerked many a knife out of my pocket and thrown it away on that account."

Youngblood laughed, and told him if he wasn't careful he would get killed before his time, yet—a jesting speech, which was destined to come true, as he was afterward hung for murder in Warrensburg, Missouri. He protested his innocence, and Youngblood always believed in it, as, except for his cowardice, there was no harm in him.

After Daniels' departure, Youngblood hired a man named George Johnson, which proved to be a jump from the frying-pan into the fire, for Johnson was a bigger coward, if possible, than Daniels, and lacked the latter's willing good-nature. The partnership, however, was of short duration, for about twenty days after it was formed an accident happened that caused it to be broken.

They had taken a load of meat into the station, and were selling it out to the emi-

grants. With some of these Johnson struck up an acquaintance, and was never weary of boasting to the young women he met of the doughty deeds he had accomplished—killing buffalo, riding wild horses, and many other things of which he knew nothing whatever. Once, while he was telling them what a splendid horseman he was, one of them said: "Dear me, I wish you would ride one of Pa's horses; no one can manage him, and he throws everyone who gets on his back."

Johnson was in a fix, but he made up his mind that it would not do to back down, so, though inwardly quaking, he answered that he could ride anything, he didn't care what it was. The horse was therefore saddled and brought out. By the time all things were in readiness for the show to begin, a large crowd, of both sexes, all ages and sizes, had gathered together to witness the fun and applaud the marvelous feats of horseman-ship. Johnson climbed into the saddle, and told the men who were at the horse's head to let him go. No sooner was this injunction

10

obeyed than the animal began to rear and plunge fearfully, and after a few jumps changed to the old trick of bucking and kicking. All at once he gave a sudden jump and came down stiffly on his fore legs, at the same time jerking his head down to the ground and kicking as high as he could with his hind legs. This was too much for a horseman of even Johnson's vaunted skill and experience, and he flew over the horse's head, with legs, arms, and fingers spread out like a jumping-jack. As he went over, the seat of his pants caught on the horn of the saddle, and remained there, being torn completely away from the garment of which it was such an important part. The unfortunate victim of his own vanity struck the ground on all fours, and full of fear that the horse would kick him, he scrambled off as fast as he could on his hands and knees, with that portion of his anatomy which in a beef is called the best steak unprotected by any other covering than that which Nature had given it. He crawled along in this way for

some distance, followed by shouts of laughter from the observers; when he finally ventured to look round, and made sure that the horse was not going to attack him, he jumped to his feet, and gathering the back part of his pants in both hands, he slunk hastily away into the bushes. It is scarcely necessary to state that he did not again appear in the presence of the young girls to whom he had boasted so loud of his prowess.

The next morning he called on Youngblood and asked him for his pay, saying that he was going to leave the country, for he would never hear the last of his misadventure if he should remain. Youngblood tried to dissuade him from his purpose, saying that the horse had thrown everybody that had tried to ride him, but it was all of no avail.

" That's all very well," he said; "but everybody has not had his breeches torn off, as I did. It's no use to talk; I won't stay."

Convinced that he meant what he said, Youngblood paid him off, and had to look out for someone else to take his place.

CHAPTER XIII.

WILD HORSES — PERISHING OF THIRST — WATER AT LAST—BONES ON THE PLAINS —KNEW MORE THAN THE GUIDE—THE RESULT OF PIGHEADEDNESS.

After he parted with Johnson, Youngblood formed a partnership with two young men named Stanfield. At that time there were a great many wild horses in the neighborhood, and the new combination decided to try their luck in catching them. It was not long after they started out that they struck a drove of about seventy-five going west. As no one of the three had had any experience in that particular line of hunting, they had no idea how far the sport was likely to carry them, and followed the horses closely, expecting to get back that night, but instead of that, they were led a long chase of about 140 miles. As they had started out without the slightest anticipation of anything of this sort, they had made no preparations for it, were without provisions, and were compelled to do entirely without water. On the second day, our friend Youngblood got accidentally separated from his two companions, and on the third day, not having tasted a drop of water for over forty-eight hours, he came to a dry branch. He dismounted from his horse, and began scratching in the mud for the longed-for fluid. While thus engaged, his horse broke loose from him, and before he could prevent it, galloped away across the prairie. He was soon out of sight, and there was Youngblood, left in the midst of the boundless prairies without food or drink, afoot and alone. He tried chewing grass to assuage his burning thirst, and he was so faint and weak that he could hardly walk, being obliged to stop and rest every few steps. He was dragging himself slowly and painfully along, and beginning to despair of escaping from his terrible predicament, when he saw, just ahead, coming toward him, a drove of wild horses. He noticed that they kept turning and looking back, as if pursued, and he soon perceived two men following them, to whom he made vigorous signs of distress. The men perceived them, and, to his great joy, rode up to him and inquired what was the matter. The two new-comers proved to be one of the Stanfield boys and a man named Reece. Youngblood's throat and tongue were so dry and parched that he could not speak, but they soon understood his dilemma. They had no water, but they gave him, a very poor substitute, some dried apples to chew and create a flow of saliva to moisten his mouth. Stanfield then took him behind him on his horse, and galloped off with him to a spring about ten miles away. It took over an hour to reach this spring, an hour of intolerable agony to our poor hero. When water was finally before him, he had to be very careful not to drink too much, taking about a pint at first, and after awhile another, and so on until he knew there was no more danger. It took a prodigious quantity to satisfy him, and it was some days before he had entirely recovered from his enforced abstinence. The horse that broke away from him was not so fortunate, but perished on the arid plains.

Many and many a man has gone out as Youngblood did, and died of hunger, thirst, or cold; it is no uncommon thing to find the bones of these unfortunates strewn over the ground where they met their miserable fate. Youngblood once found the skeleton of a man who must have frozen to death, for there were ashes near by, which showed that he had burned his wagon and even his gun-stock. He could not have been long dead, but the wolves had picked his bones completely clean. Another whose remains he discovered had a bullet-hole in his head, and, from the position of his gun, it was only too probable that he had shot himself to put an end to his sufferings. Still another was in a sitting posture, with his cloak wrapped around him, and, as there were no marks of violence on the body, had evidently perished from hunger or cold, or perhaps both together.

These are only a few instances of the hundreds who have gone to their death alone on the plains, and after the experience of terrible sufferings which no human being beheld or will ever know.

As has been said before in these pages, but the fact will bear reiteration, no person should dream of going out on the plains without a competent guide; and it will not do to take anyone that offers himself, for there are a great many men who profess to be acquainted with the country, but who know nothing about it, and such lying scamps are worse than nobody. But when a good man is procured, put your whole trust in him, and do not profess, with your limited experience, to know more than does he who has made the plains his life-study. As an illustration of the folly of persisting obstinately in having one's own way, may be cited a little experience of Youngblood's. He was hunting near Lakin Station, on the Atchison & Topeka Railroad, when a couple of men sought his services as a guide across the country to the south of the Arkansas River. A bargain was soon struck, and the journey was begun. Youngblood had his saddle-horse, and the two travelers were the possessors of a good team of mules. They proceeded about twenty miles the first day, and camped at night on the banks of a small lake. Before starting the next morning, Youngblood strongly advised his employers to fill a barrel they had in the wagon with water, as it was twenty-five miles to the next spring or lake on their route. But they said no, it wouldn't be worth while; they could stand it, and, besides, the water would soon get warm and be unfit to drink. So they contented themselves with gulping down as much as they could, and announced themselves ready to start, doubtless under the impression that they would not be thirsty any more that day; but in this they were sadly mistaken. It was intolerably hot, and they were obliged to travel under a broiling sun; so, about 11, they began to want a drink, and insisted upon driving out of the

route to examine old, dry lakes, in the hope
of finding water. Youngblood protested
against these proceedings, assuring them
that they were only losing time; that the
nearest water was the lake he had spoken of,
and that they would be able to slake their
thirst sooner by driving directly there than
by the useless exploration of dry lakes.
They finally ended by growing angry, and
told him sharply that he did not know what
he was talking about; that they knew more
about the country than he did, and that
there was no water within forty miles of
them. They became so obstinate, and even
insulting, that Youngblood could bear it no
longer, and, telling them that they might go
to a warmer country, for all he cared, rode
off and left them. After he had ridden away
a short distance, he looked back to find out
if they were following him, but saw that they
had turned, as if to return to Lakin.
Lakin was only about twenty miles in a
straight line, and about thirty-five the way
they had come; but to go directly there, one

would be forced to cross over a range of
sand-hills, which were almost impassable.
The men were in a hurry to get back, however, and, trusting to their knowledge of the
country, took the direct route, and, of
course, ran straight into the sand-hills, from
which, after floundering about all that night
and the next day, they finally emerged about
thirty miles from the place they intended to
strike. Here, fortunately for them, they
found water; but their mules had given out
before they had gotten through the hills,
and they had been obliged to leave their
wagon and foot it the rest of the way.
After they had rested, they gave a pilot $5
a day to go back with them after their
wagon; and at last, worn out and disgusted,
they reached Garden City. Here, they had
" powerful tales " to tell of the mischances
they had suffered, and pitched right and
left into their old fool of a guide for getting
them into such scrapes.

"Who was your guide?" asked an old
hunter.

"A man named Youngblood."

The hunter roared with laughter.

"Why, you donkeys," he said, "that man knows every puddle on the plains. He is A No. 1, and if you had stuck to him would have brought you out all right. All your trouble came from your pigheadedness in thinking that you knew more than your guide."

CHAPTER XIV.

One of the biggest and most exciting buf-
falo-hunts that our friend Youngblood was
ever engaged in, happened in this way: A
certain New Yorker was called West on business, and as he had a few days of spare time,
he concluded that he would like a buffalo-
chase. He had never seen a buffalo, but had
a great desire to do so, and, just for the fun
of it, to kill a dozen or two. He mentioned
his wish to the landlord of the hotel where
he was staying, a man named Potter, and
this worthy suggested Youngblood to him
as just the man likely to suit him. The
hunter being approached on the subject,
inquired how they proposed to go, remark-
ing that if it was to be on foot, he would
rather be excused. The New Yorker, how-

ever, promised to take a two-horse carriage
and a fine span owned by Potter, and Youngblood agreed to go as pilot for $3 a day.
All arrangements were soon completed, and
they started out, taking the landlord with
them.

They crossed the Arkansas River, went
about thirty miles south, and camped for the
night near the north fork of Cimarron Creek.
The next day, after driving about twenty
miles, they struck game. The landlord
wanted to show what he could do, and
declared that he could drive close up to the
herd. Youngblood let him have his way,
and, with the New Yorker, took his seat in
the back part of the carriage, where they
would have a good chance to shoot. Potter
lashed his horses without mercy, while the
other two sat patiently waiting until they
got within range; but, alas! the looked-for
opportunity never came, for, after running
at full speed, the horses became winded and
had to stop. While halting, and after the
team had became somewhat refreshed, a great

herd of buffalo, which no man's eye could
number, hove in sight about two miles away.
This time the old hunter took charge, and
some lively shooting ensued. When the
buffalo had passed, four were lying on the
ground dead, or apparently so. One was on
its back, and as the party approached, Potter remarked that he had "given that one
h—l;" but as a closer examination revealed
no blood, and, furthermore, the animal was
breathing rather lively for a dead buffalo,
Youngblood conjectured that it had been
knocked into the ditch by the others and had
been unable to get out. He took the precaution, therefore, to observe it at a point a few
feet away, as he was expecting it to make a
mighty effort and get on its feet in a way
that would make it unsafe to be too near it;
and the result proved that he was right,
for in a few moments the animal, summon-
ing all its strength, floundered, plunged, and
finally gained its feet, causing a general scat-
tering among its captors, who, however,
recovered from their alarm in time to per-

11

forate it with bullets before any damage was done. During the commotion, the herd stampeded, and the horses, becoming frightened, mixed with them, and ran fully three miles before they got clear and stopped. When the horses were recovered, Potter proposed to make another raid upon the herd, but Youngblood objected, as they already had more meat than they could carry back with them, and he disliked to see it wasted. The New Yorker, however, was anxious to go, so, leaving Youngblood to dress the four they had already killed, he and Potter started out again after the herd, which had begun to get together again. In about four hours they returned with thirty-six buffalo-tongues, having left the carcasses to rot upon the plains. This was unquestionably splendid luck, but it annoyed Youngblood that there should be such a useless waste of meat. The New Yorker, however, did not care for this, but was so overjoyed with his achievement that he said he wouldn't take $1,000 for the sport he had had.

While out on this three days' trip, they saw large numbers of wild horses, and on their return, Youngblood happened to speak of them to a man named Boslen, who became considerably interested, and finally asked the hunter what he would charge to catch some of them for him. The latter answered that he did not own enough saddle-horses for such a chase; but Boslen promised to furnish as many horses and men as he wanted, and offered him $5 a day if he would go. After some deliberation, Youngblood decided that he did not care to go in that way, for if he should fail to catch any, his employer might accuse him of not trying; but he told Boslen that if he would give him six saddle-horses, two good hands, pay all expenses, and pay him $5 a head for all he could catch, he would go. To this proposition the other readily agreed, and the bargain was concluded forthwith. The horses were selected, and the preparations for the new chase were soon made. Several droves were found before one was struck that suited them. The drove that it was finally concluded to tackle was one that Youngblood had seen many times before when out after buffalo, and he was well acquainted with their range. They went as close as they dared, and, after carefully examining them through a pair of field-glasses, Boslen declared that they would do. The first thing to be done now was to select a place for the camp as near as possible to the center of the range of the drove, for wild horses, when chased, seldom or never leave their range, although this may sometimes embrace hundreds of square miles. It is necessary, therefore, for the hunter to know the range and establish his headquarters near the center of it, where fresh horses for the chasers must always be kept in readiness.

The point that Youngblood decided to be the best for the base of his operations was his old familiar camping-place on Cimarron Creek, about thirty miles west from where they then were. This he chose as the most suitable place, both because it was near the center of the range of his game and because there was plenty of good water there, while, in most places, the lakes were nearly dried up, and the little water that was left was fast disappearing. So the next morning Boslin and the two men started for the camping-place, while our hunter rode off in pursuit of the wild horses. His mount was a good one, and he was soon quite close to the drove. When his intended prey perceived him, some of them elevated their heads and stood like equine statues, watching his every movement, while others, with their tails reared in the air, and taking a long, high trot, moved round among their companions, whinnying as if asking for counsel. As the hunter came nearer and nearer, the whole herd began to circle around him, with their heads turned toward him. Occasionally one would stop to get a better look at him, and, after satisfying his curiosity, would snort loudly and move on with the rest. Youngblood reined in his horse, and sat perfectly motionless, waiting for

them to move off, which, after making half
a dozen circles or so, they finally did, going
west, toward the place where he. had told
Boslen to fix their headquarters. He followed them as fast as he could, but, as they
were going at full speed, in spite of his best
endeavors, he could only just manage to
keep them in sight.   Shortly after they started, they struck into a wagon-road, called the
Doby Wall Trail, and, following it, passed
close to the camp.   Youngblood was anxious
to change horses, but he knew that it was
too soon for his companions to have arrived,
so he kept on in pursuit.   His plan was to
chase them down and capture the whole
drove.   He might have followed them for
awhile, and then dashed in   and lassoed a
few, but this would not have satisfied his
ambition.   He was aware that as the wild
horse gets tired, he grows tamer, and, if
the would-be captor has suitable headquarters, where he can procure fresh mounts,
so as not to give a drove much rest, the
whole herd can be easily caught.

After passing the proposed camping-place, the horses proceeded westward to the Kansas-Colorado State line; here they turned to the south, and kept this course until they struck the south fork of Cimarron Creek, where they turned to the east, passing the camp again, this time to the south. Youngblood took advantage of this to change steeds, and was after them again with more vigor than ever. They made their way east to the place where he had first started them. Here he met two men who had lost their way two days before, and, as the sky was cloudy, had been unable to find their bearings. They were nearly starved, and begged for something to eat. On the frontier, it is always customary to divide, when there is anything to divide, so Youngblood gave them a biscuit apiece, half of all he had, told them which way to go, and resumed his chase. The drove did not seem disposed now to go anywhere near the camp, but galloped back and forth across the country, between Wild Horse and White lakes. This little proceeding did not please our friend at all, for his nag was getting fagged, and if he should be forced to go all the way to camp to change, it would give the wild horses a chance to rest, and he would lose nearly, if not quite, all that he had accomplished in two days' hard work. Just as he was trying to make up his mind what to do, as good luck would have it, he fell in with a cow-boy, who, for a consideration of $5, agreed to go to the camp and tell Boslen to send a fresh horse to meet him on the old Santa Fé trail. The horses were now getting pretty well tired, and, almost directly after the meeting with the cow-boy, they turned and started off in the direction of Cimarron Creek.

Youngblood passed that night within ten miles of camp, and started bright and early the next morning to intercept the men who were to bring the horse. He struck the Santa Fé trail just in the nick of time, and after refreshing the inner man, he mounted the new horse, a strong, powerful beast, and was off once more on the chase He found

his wild horses near the place where he had left them, and, to his delight, as it showed that they were pretty well tuckered out, found most of them lying down. These animals are possessed of the most wonderful endurance, as will be seen from the fact that that night one of the mares gave birth to a colt, which traveled with the rest all the next day. About an hour after sunset, Youngblood halted for the night, knowing the colt would keep the herd near by. By this time he had them so cowed and worried by their hard, continuous racing over the country, that they grazed all around him during the night, and when he awoke the next morning he found nearly all of them lying down, stretched out as if dead. He had no mercy on them, however, but started them off again. They were evidently very stiff and sore, and they moved slowly away in a westerly direction into Colorado, where they took nearly the same route as before, turning south and then east, back into Kansas. When their indomitable hunter stopped for the night, he knew that he must be some-where near camp, but it was so dark and cloudy that he could see no signs of it. In the morning, however, he found that his surmises were correct, and that he was within half a mile of his friends, much nearer, even, than he had supposed. He found them all asleep, but soon waked them up. After a good breakfast, he took another horse and went back to look up the herd. This time he took one of the men with him to take care of the colt when it should give down, which he knew would happen in a very short time now.

He found the horses so sore and worn out that they were quite docile, and he could lead them about in almost any direction he pleased. At night he had them back again near the camp, and he told Boslen to be ready to start with them the next day for Lakin Station; but when morning came, he decided it would be safer to tire them out a little bit more, and when he finally did undertake to drive them in, he took a direct line for the station, across the sand-hills.

They were two days in crossing the hills, during which time the horses were absolutely without water, and when a lake was finally reached, they drank to repletion, from the effects of which eight of them died, a loss of $40 to Youngblood. The rest were driven some twelve miles to a cow-corral, where they were corraled, closed in, and taken across the river to Lakin, where the whole drove, twenty-four head, was safely housed.

CHAPTER XV.

His good luck in his first chase after wild horses inspired Youngblood to try it again; so he wrote to Missouri for his son and son-in-law to come out and join him, and in the meantime allowed the saddle-horses to rest and recuperate. The two young men arrived in a few days, and the three started out again south of the Arkansas River. When they reached the region of Wild Horse Lake, they found that it had been raining very heavily and the lakes were all full, so Young-blood told the boys to establish a camp about ten miles west of Wild Horse Lake, while he himself went in pursuit of a herd of seventy-two horses which they had discovered. He drove them for twelve days, but at the end of that time the provisions ran low, and it became necessary to send one of the boys back to the station for the necessaries of life. While he was preparing for the expedition, a herd of buffalo came in sight, so Youngblood ordered the horses to be put into the wagon, so that he might procure a load of meat to send into the station; but as they were going out after the buffalo, he discovered a band of Indians, about three miles away, coming toward them.

Youngblood Junior was just about to go after a young antelope, but his father stopped him, as there was no telling whether the Indians were friendly or not, and he wanted to be prepared for any emergency. He explained to the boys that it was possible that they might have to fight, and warned them to keep cool and not get excited. He then ordered them to get all the ammunition together, while he went out to reconnoiter and see how the land lay. Accordingly, he walked 200 or 300 yards away from the camp, and took up a position where he could watch the movements of the Indians. They came down into the bed of the creek, which was about a mile wide, and disappeared from sight. Youngblood now shifted his position, so that he could see them the moment they emerged into view. They came out about half a mile away from him, and were evidently surprised when they discovered the little camp. They immediately halted, gathered together in a close group, and seemed to be holding a consultation. Youngblood showed himself, and signaled to them to find out what tribe they belonged to, but they paid no attention whatever. He then signaled to know if they were friendly and what they wanted, but with no more success than formerly; his signals remained unanswered. He recognized at once that they meant no good, and hurried back to camp. He had scarcely time to get things in readiness, when he perceived that the Indians had formed, and were about to make an attack. The moment they started, he lay down flat on his stomach, and leveled his gun, prepared to drop the foremost as soon as he was near enough; but the Indian perceived his intention, and whirling his horse about, galloped back. The next followed him, and the next in like manner, until the whole band was out of range, when they stopped and held another council. Youngblood climbed up to the top of his wagon to keep an eye on them, and saw that they were preparing to surround the camp. The hill was in the shape of a half-circle, and their plan was to go around back of it, and surprise the hunters by an attack from an unexpected place. As soon as Youngblood recognized their intentions, he told the boys to jump into the wagon and drive to the top of the hill as fast as they could, so as to intercept the red-skins. He himself sprang on his saddle-horse and dashed away to the summit, where the whole game at once became evident. They were coming round the hill, stationing one of their number about every 100 yards, and in a short time the whole place would have been surrounded. Youngblood threw himself off his horse, and crawled cautiously up to the crest

of the hill, where he could have picked off
an Indian at every shot; but before he
had a chance to fire, they saw him, and
recognizing that they were beaten, threw
themselves flat upon their horses and dashed
away, not stopping until they were entirely
out of sight.

They did not leave the hill that night, but
picketed their horses and remained there till
morning.   Youngblood knew that there
would be no further attack that night, but
the boys were sure that they would get their
hair lifted, and in the morning were afraid
to go back to camp alone, so Youngblood
accompanied them, and after laying in a
good stock of provisions, started out to see
what had become of the wild horses.   These
were found without difficulty, and Youngblood followed them, with various ups and
downs, for fifteen days, at the end of which
time they were tamed and docile.   He then
got one of the boys to help him, and began
to drive them toward the station.   He had
had a long chase, and his saddle-horses were

12

considerably jaded, so much so that when within about thirty-five miles of the station, he found that he would have to have fresh ones. There was nothing to be done except to leave the boys to manage as well as they could, while he rode forward, and procuring three fresh horses, returned to find them a little nearer than when he had left them. Everything went well until they attempted to corral them, in order to get them across the river. The horses were afraid to go into the corral, and could not be persuaded to do so, and so Youngblood gave it up as a bad job, and swam them across the river. He was a little afraid to attempt the experiment, but it turned out all right, and the next day he drove sixty-nine head into the station. This was a remarkably good haul; but catching wild horses was, on the whole, by no means desirable work, and did not pay as well as one would suppose, as it was a long, wearisome job to capture a drove, and the horses being, as a rule, small and scrawny, sold for almost nothing.

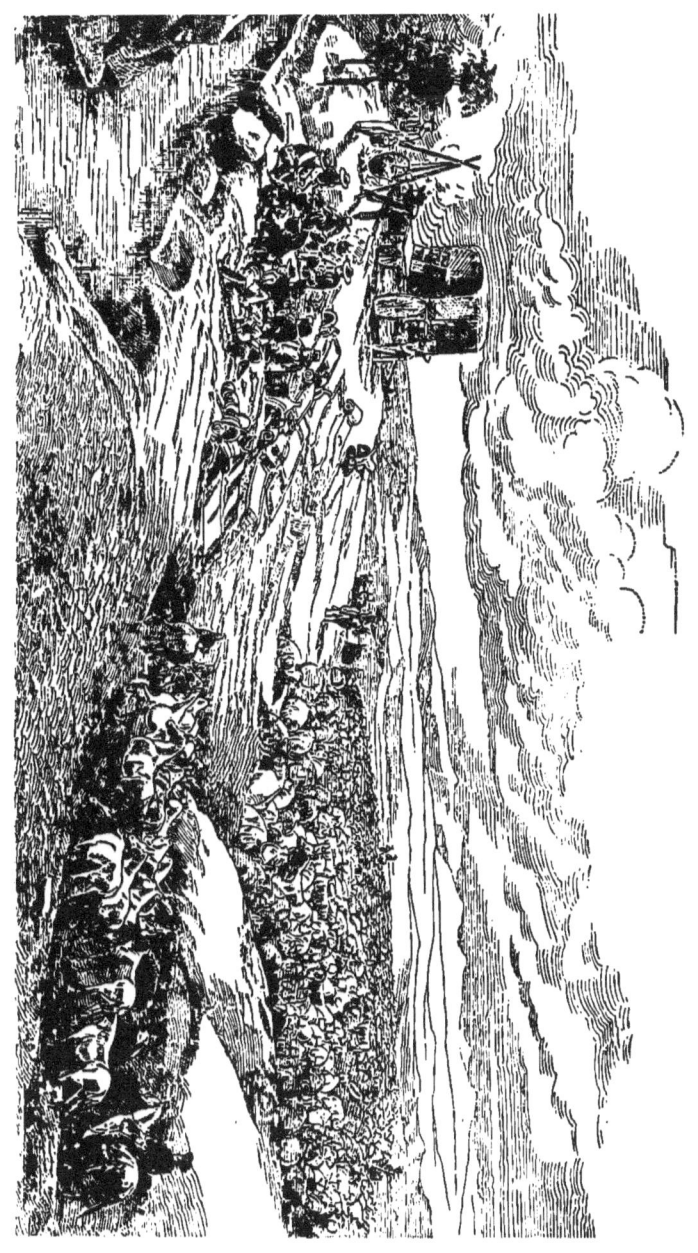

This was our hunter's last wild horse chase for that season, for it suited him much better to hunt buffalo, and he managed to procure a contract to furnish meat for the hotels.

He sent his sons home, and hired a man named Black to go with him; but the Indians proved so troublesome that he only remained with him a few days, and Youngblood was left to hunt alone. He established his camp upon the Pawnee River, right on the old Indian trail, and went to work to see what he could accomplish single-handed. The first night he was left alone he began to have fears of the Indians, and during the night these fears grew upon him more and more, until he found it impossible to dismiss them. His apprehensions banished sleep, and the next morning he was up bright and early, and shifted his quarters to a place about three miles back on the river, but still on the trail. Somehow, however, he did not feel much safer there than he did before, so he hitched up his horses and drove to the top of a hill about a mile and a half further on.

Here he halted, and looking round to see what he could see, discovered, a couple of miles to the northeast, something moving toward him. At first he thought it was buffalo, but in another moment he saw that it did not move like buffalo, and as the mass came nearer, he became aware that it consisted of mounted men, and he knew at once that it was a band of Indians moving toward him, and began to make preparations to give them a warm reception. He knew that the only show for him was to make a fight for it, and he began to seek for a position that would give him the most advantage possible. The most suitable spot for a fight that he could see was a somewhat elevated place about a quarter of a mile to his left. Here he posted himself, and commenced filling his empty cartridges. The Indians were rapidly approaching, and it seemed to him that his fingers were heavy as lead, and that, though he was working for dear life, he never made such slow progress before. There were, fortunately, only six of the red-skins, and he was confident that, with anything like a fair show, he would escape with a whole skin. He lay close until they were about 200 yards off, when he rose and waved his frying-pan at them. With a yell, they dashed toward him, and although he motioned to them to stop, they paid no attention, but kept on at a break-neck pace. Dropping on one knee, he rested his gun on the other, and leveled it at the foremost. At this maneuver they whirled with their horses sideways toward him, and throwing themselves over on their saddles on the farthest side, hung over so that Youngblood could not see them at all.

Occasionally they would peep over their horses' withers, to see what he was doing, and to watch for an opportunity to rush upon him unawares. For some minutes Youngblood and his opponents remained in this relative position, when suddenly the Indians slipped off their ponies on the opposite side, careful to keep their bodies protected, but with an eye upon the hunter and his rifle all the while. Still holding his gun in a position to cover any one of them in an instant, Youngblood called out to know what tribe they belonged to, but the only answer he could obtain was "Yah!"

"Shriam?" he asked.

"Yah!" came the answer.

"Are you Ogallahs, Arrapahoes, Utes, or what?"

The same unvarying reply was wafted back to him. He then lowered his gun, but still held it so he could bring it into position at once. The Indians now began to separate, and moved to the right and left as though they intended to surround him. He motioned them with his gun to stay together, and they responded by gestures, signifying that they were hungry and wanted something to eat. Youngblood was pretty confident that this was only a trick to get him off his guard, so he moved cautiously toward the wagon, at the same time watching them very narrowly to surprise any suspicious movement on their part. He had taken only a few steps when one of them made a rush toward him, the most unfortunate action of his life, for, in less time than it takes to tell it, there was a sharp report—the Indian with a cry of "Ow! ow! ow!" covered his face with his hands and fell lifeless to the ground. Youngblood, with an imperious gesture, motioned the others to come to him, but warned them to keep close together, so that he could cover them with his gun.   They came forward, leaving their guns hanging on their saddles, in pretense of friendship. When they were within perhaps fifteen paces, he ordered them to halt, an order they at once, obeyed, but expressed a desire to shake hands, constantly repeating, "How, how, how!"

Our friend found himself in a decidedly delicate position, for they could, if they had chosen, easily have overpowered him by mere force of numbers; they were sure, however, that some of them would have to pay the penalty with their lives, and therefore did not care to make an open attack, but pre-ferred to take him at a disadvantage, if possible. Youngblood, on his side, could easily have shot one or more of them down, but he was afraid to do so, for he did not know what effect such an action might have on the survivors. It might terrify them so that they would run away, or it might exasperate them and cause them to attack and overpower him, which would be no difficult matter in the end, although he was determined to sell his life at the dearest possible price. It was the most trying time our hero ever experienced, and he can not look back on it now without a shudder. For more than an hour he held them at arm's, or rather gun's, length, when they gave up all hope of trying to shake hands with him, and began to try to steal back to their guns. But Youngblood was alive to the situation, and when one of them would make a move toward his horse, he instantly covered him and ordered him back to the squad. He noticed that one of them was doing his best to assume a careless air, and seemed to be aimlessly twirling a lariat which he held in his hand. After

swinging it round for awhile, he let it slip,
apparently by accident, and one end of it fell
at the white man's feet. Here he let it lie
for a moment, and then began winding it up;
but, instead of drawing the rope toward him,
he followed it, gradually approaching nearer
and nearer his enemy. Youngblood was too
cunning and too well versed in Indian tac-
tics not to understand this maneuver. He
knew it was no time for dilly-dallying, and
he at once put a stop to the proceeding by
an action which at the same time finished
the existence of the wily strategist. The
others, under cover of the smoke, sprang to
their horses and hurried away, quickly disappearing on the horizon, leaving their con-
queror weak and faint from the long-
continued strain that had been imposed upon
him. A little later in the day, this same
band ran across a man named Matthews,
who, with two other men, was driving a herd
of cattle, and, by an appearance of the
greatest friendship, succeeded in throwing them off their guard. After shaking

hauds with them in the most cordial manner, they asked for something to eat—an Indian, by the way, is always hungry—and partook liberally of what was offered them. But they were only waiting for an opportunity, and no sooner did it appear than they shot two of their hosts down. Matthews, the survivor, sprang on his horse and dashed away in time to save his life, but not, however, without receiving a severe bullet wound in the shoulder from a shot sent after him as he was fleeing.

This incident in itself is sufficient to show the treacherous nature of the red man of the forest, and how worthless are his professions of friendship. Youngblood declares that he never saw one that he could trust, and he firmly believes that his suspicions have more than once saved his life. The only Indians that he ever saw that were not dangerous were dead ones.

CHAPTER XVI.

DISAPPOINTMENT—BAD WEATHER—FRIGHT-
ENING A SCHOOL—A CLOSE SHAVE.

After his little experience with the Indians, Youngblood determined to stay alone no longer, and immediately went across to Silver Lake to join an old hunter who was encamped there, and whose equal in a scrimmage with red-skins it was hard to find. Many an Indian had dropped at the crack of his rifle, and he was well known among them and as universally feared as he was known. The two of them together, at ten minutes' notice, could have made it decidedly warm for any number of reds that were likely to attack them; but, to our friend's intense disappointment, when he arrived at the camp he found that the hunter had gone into the station, and he was compelled to remain alone after all, with the Indians in

close proximity every day. He continued
hunting for some time, however, without
being molested by them, although he managed to get into some other scrapes that
were not much pleasanter than an Indian
fight.

One day, when he was out hunting, the sky
clouded over, and a cold rain set in, which
lasted forty-eight hours, completely soaking
his blankets and chilling him to the bone.
When the weather cleared, he went out for
game, and, after going about four miles,
found two large buffalo and succeeded in
dispatching them both. It was still very
cold for October, had clouded over again and
was beginning to snow; so he turned out
his team, and, after dressing the animals
which he had killed, he dragged them close
together, back to back, laid his blankets over
them, and on top of the blankets spread the
green hides with the hairy side down; he
then crawled in between the hides and blankets and lay there for two days, until the storm
was over. It was warm enough, but it was

impossible to make a fire, and all that he had
to eat were a few handfuls of flour. While
he lay there the buffalo swarmed all around
him, and, as soon as the weather allowed,
he commenced to scatter them. He killed
two, and, loading the four on his wagon,
drove through the slushy roads, for the snow
was now melting, to the place where he had
camped during the rain-storm, and discovered that a band of Indians had been there,
and had but recently left. It was a narrow
escape, but "a miss is as good as a mile,"
and there was no use in getting frightened
after the danger was all over. This particular spring was a famous camping place, directly on the Indian trail, but as much
frequented by white men as by red-skins.
He thought he might find some game further
on, and, with this end in view, drove for several miles, but without success, and so concluded to return to town with what he
already had. As he repassed the spring, he
saw that a squad of Indians were in possession. The only reason he would have for

stopping would be to obtain water, but as the melted snow was entirely sufficient to quench his thirst, there was no occasion to run the risk of a fight, and he passed them about half a mile away.

About a mile further on, he discovered three buffalo lying with their backs toward him. At first he hesitated about killing them, for the report of his gun would probably apprise the unsuspecting Indians of his whereabouts; but the temptation was too great, and, driving as near as he dared, he took his gun and stole cautiously toward them. When he was close upon them, to his horror he discovered three red-skins coming up on the other side. They perceived him at almost the same time, and for some minutes they stood perfectly still, watching each other. Youngblood, however, soon grew tired of the inaction, and advanced again on the buffalo, keeping one eye on the Indians as he did so. As soon as the animals rose to their feet, he shot them down one after the other. He then brought up his wagon, and placing it between himself and the Indians, who had squatted down on the ground and were calmly watching his proceedings, began skinning the game, but without relaxing his vigilance. The red-skins did not seem to be disposed to any act of hostility, and he finished his work, loaded the meat on his wagon, and drove away without being in the slightest degree disturbed.

On his arrival in Sherlock, he found the town in the greatest excitement over the Indian outrages and the killing of General Custer and his command, which was an event of recent occurrence. As Youngblood had been out so long, his friends felt certain that he had met with a fate similar to the one which had befallen that gallant band. Uncle Sam had kindly fed and fattened the red devils until they were in excellent fighting trim and were ready for all atrocities. In dozens of localities people had been surprised by them and shot down like wild beasts; some, moreover, being tortured and mutilated in the most revolting manner, and others scalped and left to die a lingering death. In one place they attacked a school presided over by a lady teacher. They did not kill any of the pupils, for a wonder, but satisfied themselves with frightening them almost to death. They pulled their hair, thumped them, banged them, pretended to tomahawk them, and yelled with laughter when the terrified girls begged for their lives. Three young ladies of the school were strip-ped entirely naked and told to go home in that condition. After sufficiently amusing themselves, the fiends left, but the outraged people rose *en masse* in pursuit. The Indians had stolen a great many horses and cattle, and the cowboys, who are more than a match for the reds and delight in fighting them, were especially eager in their desire for vengeance. So keen was the chase that when the devils saw their chief, Sitting Bull, again, it was with greatly depleted ranks.

The troops finally came to the relief of the people, but there is so much red tape in

all their actions that they nearly always move too slow to catch Indians. Good work in this raid, however, should be credited to Colonel Lewis, who, with several of his men, was killed in an engagement on White Woman Creek. When this deplorable affair took place, Youngblood was hunting on the same creek, but he did not take much part in the fighting, as he was of the opinion that if the Government fed and fattened the Indians, and employed soldiers to kill them when in good condition, it was as well to allow those whose business it was to attend to it, to do so. Still, although he took no active part in the hostilities, his business brought him into frequent collision with the red-skins, but all the fighting he did was purely a matter of self-defense, and he made it a point not to indulge in any unnecessary conflict.

One evening, a few days after the battle on White Woman Creek, Youngblood, who was out with a man named Frank Howard, saw something in a side draw of the creek

13

which he supposed to be buffalo, but the air
was so filled with smoke that he could not
distinguish to a certainty. When within about half a mile, he found, by aid of his
field-glass, that it was a band of Indians
lying on the ground, holding their horses by
their bridles. This was somewhat alarming,
and our hunter began to fear that they had
scouts stationed all about. He told Howard
that the best thing to be done was to with-
draw a few hundred yards to a ravine or
washout, and remain there for the night.
This was a good position, and would afford
them a fair opportunity to repel any attack
that might be made upon them. They hurried their supper and put out the fire as soon
as possible, that it might not betray their
position. They then made the best preparations for defense they could, and sat down
to watch and wait. Shortly after dark, the
dog, with an incessant barking and growling,
began to dash savagely up and down the
ravine, and then run back with his tail between his legs, thoroughly frightened.

From these actions, Youngblood knew that the Indians were prying about the camp with no good intent, and he warned his companion to be in readiness to go to work at a moment's notice. It was too dark and smoky to see any great distance, so how near the enemy really was there was no way of telling. After a while the dog quieted down, and then the two men took turns in watching during the night. As soon as it was light, they examined the ground around the camping place, and found that the Indians had been within twenty paces of them. They were a remnant of the band that had fought with Lewis a few days before, and probably made no attack upon the two hunters because they were dodging the soldiers, and were anxious to escape from that part of the country.

The whites were not the only ones to suffer during this outbreak, for the Indians were compelled to undergo severe privations. As an example, when they were scattered in the fight on White Woman, an old squaw and a pappoose about seven years old could not get away, and, to avoid being captured, hid themselves in a washout.   When the soldiers left they did not know what to do or where to go, as their tribe was broken up, and so they remained where they were. They could obtain plenty of water, but there was nothing to eat except the carcasses of the animals that had been slain during the fight, and so severe was their hunger that when, after some time, they were discovered and taken prisoners to Fort Dodge, they had almost entirely eaten up a mule, the flesh of which was horribly putrefied, and the squaw and child emitted an odor scarcely less overpowering.

CHAPTER XVII.

ENGLISHMEN ON A LARK—BETTER SHOTS AT
BEER-BOTTLES THAN BUFFALO—A TUSSLE
WITH A CALF—HOWARD IN TROUBLE—
DODGING A DETECTIVE.

It was not long after the Indian outbreak
that five Englishmen came to Lakin Station
on a lark. They were not peers of the realm,
dukes, marquises, or earls, but honest,
healthy, well-bred inhabitants of the "right
little, tight little island," who had come to
this country on a sight-seeing tour, and were
determined to have a good time. They had
plenty of money, and spent it right royally,
having their fun and paying for it, too.

Their object in coming to Lakin was to have
a buffalo-hunt on the plains, and who better
could be found to lead them on that amusement than the old and experienced scout and
hunter, Youngblood. As they intended to
do the shooting themselves (they were pro-

vided with the best of guns—a rifle and a
shotgun apiece), he consented to act as their
guide for $5 a day, which they pronounced
cheap enough.

A two-horse carriage was procured, and
a full stock of provisions and ammunition laid in. Youngblood did not ride in
the carriage, but took his own wagon and
team, so as to be ready for business when
they got tired of paying their $5 a day.

From Lakin they drove in a northeasterly
direction; and when about twenty miles out,
the Englishmen received their first sensation
in the shape of a large rattlesnake, which
they were greatly interested in. Youngblood
made it "sing" for them, and when he finally
killed it, one of them kept the skin to be
made into a hat-band. Then they all proceeded to take a swig of beer, of which they
had brought a large quantity, and made a bet
as to who could break the bottle when tossed
up into the air. Finally one succeeded, and
they reëntered the carriage, ready to proceed
with the journey; but they had only gone a

short distance, when one of them, who had his head out of the window, exclaimed, "Lord, look there!" and called out to the driver to stop. Youngblood supposed, of course, that he had discovered a buffalo or something of that sort; but not being able to perceive any himself, followed the direction of the Englishman's eyes, and saw that the object over which he was almost going into hysterics was a large specimen of terrapin. They all clambered out, turned the novel beast over with their boots, poked it with their guns, and, after they were satisfied, drank another bottle, made a bet as to who could hit it, broke it, got into the carriage again, and drove off.

Perhaps a mile further on, four antelope came dashing by at full speed; and then there was a scene of unparalleled excitement indeed. All five of them jumped out with their guns and began firing as fast as they could. Bullet after bullet whistled through the air, and the poor antelope ran for dear life, badly scared, but not seriously injured, and probably not much more excited than the Englishmen themselves. The hunters were badly disappointed at the loss of their game, but consoled themselves by drinking another bottle and breaking it as before.

They camped for the night on a small creek, and when they arose the next morning, could see the antelope scurrying about in all directions. The animals seemed to be tolerably tame, and the pleasure-hunters kept blazing away at them as they passed until afternoon, but, to their chagrin, without any other effect than that of frightening the pretty creatures.

When they stopped for dinner, one of them, who was known among his companions by the *sobriquet* of "Calamity Jane," full of disgust at their ill success, suggested that they put "the old man," meaning Youngblood, to shooting, or otherwise they would be likely to starve before they got back to the station. "Because," he added, "we have fired five hundred shots to-day and killed nothing, and if this thing is kept up we will soon be out of ammunition and have no game

to show for it." The question was then put to vote, and it was agreed, without a dissenting voice, that their guide should kill them an antelope.

Youngblood was nothing loath, and told them if they would all stay in the carriage he thought he might, perhaps, manage to get them an antelope for supper. Long before the camping-place was reached he spied a drove, and, getting quietly out of the wagon, he slipped up as close to them as he could. He did not want to run any chances of missing, after having poked so much fun at the marksmanship of the others; so when near enough to shoot, he lay down in the grass and waited for a good opportunity. This was not slow in coming. In a few moments he had two within range, and, taking careful aim, fired, bringing both of them down at the first shot. At this the men leaped out of their carriage and came running up to the successful sportsman, more excited, if possible, than when they had fired the forty or fifty shots at the four scared beasts. After they had thoroughly examined and wondered over the first dead antelope they had ever seen, Youngblood removed the entrails, threw the carcasses upon the wagon, and the procession was resumed. The Englishmen still kept on firing at antelope, badgers, hawks, and whatever they saw, but without doing much execution, until they came to Clear Creek, where they were to camp for the night. Here they had better success, for there were ducks galore, and in duck-shooting they were, so to speak, on their native heath; and with the ducks and the antelope, the supper was a feast fit for a king.

In the morning they harnessed up again, and drove in a northwesterly direction to Bear Creek, where they camped for that night. The next day they came upon their first buffalo, a splendid herd. The English gentlemen were very anxious to kill them all, and they jumped out of the carriage and started boldly toward them, very much as if they thought the buffalo would be delighted to see them; but when they were within about a quarter of a mile of them, the animals raised their heads, and, taking a short survey, galloped off, leaving the nabobs sadly disappointed. They complained bitterly of their bad luck to Youngblood, but he could not refrain from laughing, and told them that they had done much better than he had expected, as he had thought they would frighten them away before they had got half so near.

It was with considerable reluctance, nevertheless, that they gave up the buffalo and returned, for the rest of the day, to their former occupation of firing at antelope and fowl, but with their usual luck.

That night the camp was pitched on a small creek called Rocky Branch, and, while eating breakfast in the morning, one of them said, with a rather wry face: "Mr. Youngblood, how much do we owe you?"

"Well," said the hunter, "I have been with you for five days and at $5 a day, that would make $25!"

The money was paid, and they then announced that they had done hunting, and wanted to see him shoot a little.

"All right," said Youngblood. "If you stay with me awhile, I shall probably shoot something."

They then moved about six miles, to White Woman Creek, where a large herd of buffalo was struck. Youngblood killed one the first shot, and then getting a "stand" on them, killed seven more. During the afternoon he succeeded in potting four antelope. When they stopped for the night, he cooked some of the buffalo humps for the Englishmen, who thought it the finest meat they had ever tasted. The hunter could not resist having a little fun with them on account of their shooting.

"Why," he said, "you had me for five days for $25, and got nothing, and in one day I have made twice that amount."

They took it good-naturedly, and let him joke all he wanted as they drove back to the station, where they had more of the humps

for dinner, but they did not like them as well as those Youngblood had cooked on the prairie, and finally insisted on his cooking them some more himself.

Youngblood remained but one day at the station with his English friends before bidding.them farewell and starting out again for the range with Howard, a former companion of his.

At White Woman Creek a large herd of buffalo was found. They were standing in the creek drinking, but before Youngblood could get near enough, they came out of the water and started away. He fired on them at long range, and killed a large cow. She was just going up the bank, and when the bullet struck her, she rolled down the steep bank, about twelve feet, and, falling into the soft mud, went almost entirely under. The two men worked for a long time trying to extricate her, but she was so firmly imbedded in the mud that they found it impossible to move her, gave it up as a bad job, and went on after the herd. Several shots were fired, but with little or no success, the only damage done being the breaking the shoulder of a calf about six months old. The disabled calf could not keep up with the rest, and they followed it along up the bed of a side draw until they perceived the herd had stopped to rest further up the draw. The calf had got pretty well tired out by this time, and could easily have been shot, but Youngblood did not want to alarm the herd, so he headed it off and started in to catch it. He could get tolerably close to it, but not close enough to lay hands on it, and every time it passed him, it would show fight. It was small, and, concluding that he could push it off without much difficulty, he finally stood his ground. The calf came on, shaking its head viciously, and when within a few feet of him, made a sudden dash at him like an old ram. Youngblood had no time to even raise his hands, and in another moment the calf was upon him, knocked him down, and began trampling upon him. Finding that it did not mean to let him go, he reached up, seized it by the ears, and, after quite a tussle, succeeded in throwing it off, and finished it with his knife.

After dressing it, the hunters started on after the herd, but had to follow them twelve miles before they could get a shot at them, and then only succeeded in killing one, which ran on about three hundred yards before it fell. This was on Beaver Creek, and the beavers had built a dam which made it impossible to cross with the wagon. As it was now about sundown, Youngblood told Howard to turn the horses out, and he would go over and skin the buffalo. He crossed the creek on the beaver dam, but had hardly begun dressing his game when he noticed, some three-quarters of a mile away, three men on horseback coming toward him. Thinking them to be Indians, he hurried back and told Howard to gather up the ammunition and be ready to repel an attack. It proved to be a false alarm, however, as the riders turned out to be cowboys who were hunting up some lost cattle.

For sometime past Youngblood had observed that his partner, Howard, did not seem to be in an easy frame of mind, and he concluded that he had got into trouble somewhere, and was afraid of the consequences. He had often met men of this description out on the plains, and he had let the matter pass without remarks or inquiries. But when they were about to start in this time with their load of meat, Howard grew more nervous and uneasy than ever, and was so palpably disturbed and worried that he made up his mind to speak to him about it and give him a chance to unload himself of his burden and relieve the strain upon his mind.

So, when the opportunity offered, as they were driving along, he asked him if anything was troubling him, and if he could do anything to help him.

"Do I look as if anything was bothering me?" inquired Howard, with a sorrowful smile.

"Yes, you do," answered Youngblood. "I have seen many a man in your condition,

and I can guess pretty well what is the matter with you. If you are in a difficulty and half-way innocent, I will try to help you in some way or other; and even if you are guilty of some crime, I will agree not to give you away; so spit it out, and let's see what can be done. It is my opinion that you made away with some fellow in the place where you came from; but, whatever it is, let's have it."

At these last words Howard looked utterly astounded, and, as soon as he could recover from his amazement, said, stammeringly:

"Well, you're a pretty good guesser. I am in trouble, and in the way you say, but I am not guilty of willful murder, although I confess that I dread the consequences of being caught. I'll tell you the whole truth. This is the way it happened : At Fort Scott, Missouri, I traded horses with a jockey— well, I just traded horses, that's all; but the next day he came to me and insisted that I trade back, saying that I had cheated him by lying about my horse. I told him that I
14

never traded back; when I traded and found myself cheated, I had to stand by my bargain, and, on the other hand, if I happen to make a good trade, I mean to keep it. At this he grew furious, and said he would make me trade back; but I told him that he would do nothing of the sort. Then he flew at me with his rawhide whip and began lashing me over the head and face with it. This was more than I could stand, and as he was a big bully, I drew my knife and used it with fatal effect. As soon as I realized what I had done, I hastened to make my escape—not because I was afraid of being hanged, but because I knew that to clear myself would cause me a heap of trouble and cost me a lot of money. I had no friends with me at the time, and I knew that the few spectators were reckless men and greatly prejudiced against me. But what worries me most just now is that I have sent for my family to meet me at Lakin; they will be there to-morrow or next day, and I have been thinking that the officers may follow them and trace me out in that way.

Now, Mr. Youngblood, what I want to know is this: Do you blame me for using my knife on him, and will you do anything against me?"

"No," was the prompt answer, "I do not blame you at all, if it happened the way you say, and I will do anything I can to help you; so, if you have anything you want me to do, let me hear it."

"I have nothing I want you to do just at present," he replied, "except that when we are near the station, I would like to have you go in first, if you will, and find out if there are any strangers in town. If so, try to discover if they are from Fort Scott or thereabouts, and what their business is. And, by the way, if my family should be there already, you can tell them how matters are, and let me know as soon as you can how the land lies."

Youngblood promised to fulfill his wishes, and accordingly, the next morning, went in alone. Soon after his arrival in Lakin, he noticed a stranger hanging about, but, pay-

ing no attention to him for the moment, began getting rid of his load of meat. In a few
moments the stranger came up to the wagon,
and, examining the meat, remarked carelessly that it was the first he had ever seen.

"Indeed," said Youngblood, feigning
astonishment; "why, where do you come
from?"

"From Fort Scott, near Missouri."

This was enough to convince our friend
that he was a detective hunting for Howard, and he could not help wondering at his
being so stupid as to tell where he came from,
and so giving himself away. The man
evinced much interest in Youngblood, and
followed him about, talking to him at every
opportunity.

"Let me see," he asked at last, "what
is your name?"

Youngblood saw no harm in giving that
information, and told him his name.

"Do you hunt for a living?"

"Yes."

"Do you hunt by yourself?"

"Well, sometimes I do."

"Have you anybody with you now?"

"Yes, but I don't know where he is."

"Are you going out again?"

"Yes."

"When?"

"I don't know; it depends upon circumstances. I may go out to-morrow, and I may not go out for a week or more."

"Well," said the stranger, with a sidelong glance, "if you go out to-morrow, I would like to go with you."

Youngblood calmly told him that he would see about it, and left him.

When he reached the hotel, he found that Howard's family were indeed there, but the detective, who had followed him, watched him so closely that he could find no chance to speak to Mrs. Howard. He was very roughly dressed and his clothes were bloody, and the woman, as she afterward confessed, at first took him for a desperado, reeking with the blood of his victims. As soon, however, as she found out that he was the "old hunter" whom her husband was with, she longed to speak to him, but did not dare to do so in the presence of the stranger, whom she had noticed getting on and off the cars every time she did, and had pretty well made up her mind as to his identity.

The chance came, however, at last, and Youngblood found a safe opportunity to tell her where her husband was. The poor woman begged him to help them to outwit the detective and effect their escape. He promised to do so, and, about 10 o'clock that night, he slipped out of town, went to Howard and reported what he had seen and heard, telling him to lie close until the next night, when he would try to get him away.

All the next day Youngblood strolled about the station, and spent considerable time in the company of the stranger from Fort Scott. He took care to announce in his presence that he intended to go on another hunt soon, and told him that if his partner did not return he would be glad of his (the detective's) company. The other professed himself anxious to go, and the two parted fast friends. But, alas for human calculations! When the Fort Scott man got up the next morning, he found that the woman and children he had followed so carefully from Missouri had disappeared—no one knew where.

It is needless to say that this strange vanishing was due to Youngblood. As soon as all the village was still in sleep, he had harnessed up his team, and, taking Howard's family with him, had driven to the place where the fugitive lay concealed, and started the whole party to Colorado, telling them to keep hidden during the day and travel only by night. He got back to the hotel in time for breakfast; and when the detective missed Mrs. Howard and her children, he evidently at once suspected the hunter of knowing something about the matter, for he gave him a sharp, scrutinizing look, as if he thought that he could tell how they got away, if he chose. He said nothing, however; but, as good luck would have it, some-one told him that a woman with children had boarded a train that passed through during the night; so he took the first train he could that went in the same direction, left on a false scent, and Youngblood never saw him again.

Howard was afterward caught, taken back to Fort Scott, tried, and acquitted. He is now working as a fireman on the Atchison, Topeka & Santa Fé Railroad.

CHAPTER XVIII.

Howard's enforced flight left Youngblood without a hand; but he soon procured one, a man named Henderson, who owned a good team, which, with Youngblood's own, made a capital hunting outfit. On their first expedition they went to White Woman Creek. On their way they saw hundreds of antelope, but as this was not the game they were looking for, they did not disturb them. As they could find no buffalo, they crossed the creek and camped for the night, shooting an antelope for supper.

The next day they moved on to Beaver Creek, and again stopped for the night, camping under the bluff, about twenty yards from the water. It was cool, clear weather, and the creek was very low; but when they got up in the morning, they were astounded to find themselves surrounded by water. This was all the more surprising as it had not rained a drop during the night. Strive as they would, they could not understand the phenomenon; but there was no doubt about the fact that the water had risen from four inches to six feet, and evidently this was not the result of any freshet, for the water was not in the slightest degree muddy.

They waded out, getting uncomfortably wet in the operation, and, after breakfast, proceeded down the creek to investigate the sudden rise. The cause must be some stoppage below, Youngblood thought, and, sure enough, they had not gone far when they came to a big beaver dam, which the beavers were hard at work repairing. At once the cause of the remarkable rise of the creek was explained, and the mystery was a mystery no longer. The dam had recently broken and allowed the water in the creek to run out, and the beavers had filled up the break during the night, occasioning the overflow.

It may not be out of place here, and will prove interesting to the reader, to give a short sketch of the habits of this singularly intelligent little animal.

The beaver is about three times as large as the common raccoon, with which all are familiar—usually at least two feet in length from the nose to the root of the tail. The tail, which the animals use as a trowel, is about ten inches in length and an inch thick, broad, flat, and covered with scales. They are very aquatic in their mode of life, and seldom wander far from a lake or river. Their hind feet are spread out like those of a goose, and webbed, which make them peculiarly good swimmers, and they have the power of staying a remarkably long time under water. Their teeth are heavy and pointed, and so strong that they are able to cut down large trees with them. Their houses, which are the admiration of mankind, are cone-shaped, built of sticks and mud, with the entrance under the water, and the different lodges are connected by passages. When the depth of water is not sufficient, the beavers build a dam, near which the house or lodge is placed. These dams are built of mud, sticks, logs, and even large trees—the latter cut down with their teeth, at some point above the dam, and carried to the proper place by floating them down the current. The walls of the lodges are very thick, and the whole structure is not only very warm, but affords ample protection from wolves and other beasts of prey. To one who has never seen a beaver town and dam, the sight is as wonderful and instructive an one as anything that could possibly be shown him.

Leaving the beaver dam that had been the cause of so much astonishment to them, Youngblood and his companion passed down the creek about twenty miles, and crossed to the Twin Lakes, about which they found quantities of antelope, and decided to stop right there and kill a load. Henderson turned out the horses, and Youngblood got down to work with his trusty rifle, and soon had twenty-four carcasses stretched out before him. The next morning he also obtained a large buffalo which came down to water. This made their load, both wagons being filled to repletion, and they pulled in to Sherlock, where they sold out for $71, one third of which went to Henderson.

They stayed in Sherlock only one night and were off again, this time going along the bed of the Pawnee River, where they felt pretty certain to find buffalo; but in this they were disappointed, for on their arrival they found that the Indians had been there and had chased them out of the country on horseback. To hunt them with horses frightens the buffalo badly, and when once stampeded from this cause, they do not soon stop. Finding, therefore, their hopes of buffalo vain, the partners proceeded to kill a load of antelope, which they carried to Pierceville, the nearest station.

They then took another shoot, going south to the Arkansas River. Youngblood had always found buffalo plenty in this region, and supposed he would do so again. But, as it turned out, he was no luckier than he had been at Pawnee River; for they had driven scarcely more than twenty miles south when they came to where the prairie had been recently burned, and for the two succeeding days they saw nothing but an arid waste of blackened ground. The worst of all was that they had taken very little "grub" with them, expecting to find plenty of game, but all the game had been driven away by the fire. They had two dogs with them, which soon began to manifest decided symptoms of hunger; but as they had almost nothing for themselves, they did not deem it exactly prudent to divide with their canine comrades. At last Youngblood spied a badger lying near his hole, and shot him for the dogs, but the dainty animals would not touch it. He thought they would probably get hungry enough to eat it before long, so he threw it into the wagon and took it along; when they camped that night, he offered it to them again, but they were not ready for it yet. He then dressed it and roasted it nicely, but still they would have nothing of it. He left it before them, however, and by morning the pangs of hunger got the best of them, and they devoured every atom of it.

About 2 o'clock the next day the north fork of Cimarron Creek was reached, and just as they struck the creek Henderson pointed to a hill about a hundred yards to the left of them, saying: "There are four buffalo heads; some hunter has been here not long ago."

Youngblood jumped upon the wagon to get a good look at them, but in a moment he warned his companion to squat down, for those heads were still attached to the buffalo. He took his gun, and, coming as close to them as he dared, saw that one was a cow and the other three were young ones. He concluded, therefore, to kill the cow first, as he would then be pretty apt to get them all; and this conjecture proved correct, for the old one never got up after the first bullet struck her, and in two minutes all four were dead. It is needless to state that the little party fared sumptuously that night, dogs and all.

The next day they drove ten miles, which brought them out of the burnt district. Youngblood then mounted a high hill, and, scanning the broad extent of horizon with his field-glass, discovered, about six miles ahead, a large herd of the game he was in search of. He drove as close as was possible with the wagon, and then got out, and, shooting one down, got a "stand" on the herd, and soon killed all that could be hauled in both wagons.

As they were driving into town, they saw a large herd close to the road, and, as they wished to pay them a visit in the near future, when they could take care of some of them, they drew quietly up in the shade of a clump of trees, in order not to frighten them. The buffalo soon moved out of the road, and the hunters drove rapidly to the station, where they disposed of their meat as quickly as possible, and, hiring a hand to go with them, started back for the herd they had left.

Youngblood was pretty confident that they would be found in the vicinity of Bear Creek, as they were heading in that direction, and with that expectation he drove up the creek, keeping a sharp outlook on both sides. After traveling about forty miles, however, the party were overtaken by a severe snow-storm, which left about six inches of snow on the ground, and compelled them to lay over for two days in the bed of Bear Creek.

On the morning of the third day, as Youngblood was busily engaged in making a fire, he was startled by a fearful racket close at hand. Running up a bank to find out what it all meant, he saw a buffalo fighting desperately with four ravenous wolves. The wolf, as a rule, is quite unable to contend with the buffalo; but a pack of them will often hang around a herd to devour calves which may stray, or aged animals which have become too weak to keep up with the rest, and even these are apt to deal death to many of their assailants before they are forced to yield to numbers. In this case, the buffalo

15

had been hurt in some way across the loins, and could no longer run. The wolves kept flying at it, first from one side and then the other, and tearing out great mouthfuls at each jump, in their hungry pertinacity. But they were destined never to enjoy their feast, for at the appearance of the hunter they fled howling away, leaving him in undisputed possession of the prize.

As the snow and delay had ruined all chances of finding the expected buffalo, Youngblood turned south toward the north fork of Cimarron Creek, where they ran across a herd of fourteen, of which they captured eleven. This made out the load, and they drove back to the station again.

When they arrived in Lakin, they found three men there, from New York, who had never seen a live buffalo. They examined the load of meat very curiously, and finally asked Youngblood what he would charge to let them go with him the next time he went out hunting. They said they merely wanted to go along to see the sights, and not to take

any active part in the shooting. Youngblood
told them that he would let them go for a
dollar apiece a day—terms which they were
only too glad to accept. So, as soon as everything could be got in readiness, they started
from Lakin and went south of the Arkansas
River to the head-waters of North Fork
Creek, about thirty miles back. They camped
for the night on the creek. Snow fell during
the night to the depth of about four inches,
so they were obliged to wait in the morning
until it had thawed somewhat. It was 10
o'clock before they harnessed up; they drove
about fifteen miles up the creek, when
Youngblood began to think it was about
time to strike some buffalo; so he mounted
to quite a lofty hill, where he could get a
good view for miles, and eagerly swept the
landscape with his glass. There were immense numbers of horses and cattle to be
seen in all directions, and, after gazing for
some time, he at last made out a herd of
buffalo about five miles away.

When he returned to the wagon and

informed his companions of his discovery, their joy knew no bounds, and they were all anxiety to be off at once, a desire that Youngblood himself was only too glad to gratify. They soon got on lower ground, and for some time were out of sight of the herd; but they kept steadily on their course, and when they finally came once more in sight of the buffalo, they were not more than half a mile away.

It was Youngblood's usual custom to crawl on his hands and knees through the grass until he was as near to a herd as he wished; but this time the ground was so cold and muddy that he did not feel like crawling, but just ran rapidly toward his intended game until they showed signs of alarm, and then he at once began shooting. He had to fire at very long range; but, after several shots, he managed to wound one of the animals in the shoulder. The stricken beast was soon unable to keep up with the herd, and dropped behind. The hunter waited until the wagon came up, and then he set the dogs on the crippled buffalo. The latter made its way the best it could after the herd, with the dogs at its heels worrying it, until it came to a rise in the ground, when the rest of the herd, seeing the fight, turned, and, dashing back, began to try to kill the dogs, who, although "laying at them" all the time, managed to keep out of the way.

As the fight progressed, assailants and assailed gradually moved toward the place where Youngblood and his companions stood watching the sport. The New Yorkers, when they observed this approach, began to grow alarmed; but Youngblood assured them that there was no danger, and if they would come with him he would show them how to kill buffalo. Nothing could induce them, however, to move a step closer to the dreaded beasts; and, finding it was useless to waste further words upon them, the hunter advanced to within a hundred and fifty yards of the buffalo, and began firing upon them. The herd were entirely absorbed with the dogs, and at every shot one of them dropped. Finally, there was but one left. The solitary animal suddenly became conscious of his loneliness, and, in search of company, galloped off straight toward the New Yorkers. They, poor fellows, thought sure that their last moment was come, and, with shrieks of alarm, began darting aimlessly hither and thither. Perhaps this frightened the monarch of the prairies, for he stopped to see what sort of strange animals these were. His pause was fatal to him, for in another moment he dropped with a bullet, sent by Youngblood's trusty "old poison-slinger," through his heart. The New Yorkers were immensely relieved when they saw their enemy fall, and probably believe to this day that Youngblood saved their lives, although there was really very little danger.

It wanted now only an hour to sunset, and there were thirteen buffalo to dress before bed-time. Besides the New Yorkers, Youngblood had only one person with him, a man named Lee Howard—a good hand, fortunately, who had made several trips with our hero, and knew his business. The New Yorkers offered to help, and did the best they could; but they were rather a hindrance than a help, for they were bankers' clerks and unfledged lawyers, who had never seen a buffalo. With the exception of three, the carcasses lay within a radius of thirty feet; Youngblood built a fire in the center, and by midnight the meat was dressed and safely packed away.

The party were too excited for sleep, so they talked the remainder of the night. The next morning, they saw a herd of about three hundred. Youngblood, the indefatigable, pitched in and got eight. This made all they could haul, and they started back to Lakin. When they reached the hotel, the landlord asked Youngblood why he had not brought some antelope. The latter replied that he was after buffalo and had not thought anything about antelope, but promised to go out the next day and see what he could do to satisfy the desires of mine host.

True to his promise, in the morning he

mounted his old Indian pony, and, finding a nice herd of the graceful creatures not far from the station, killed three of them. He had with him a rope about twenty feet long that he was in the habit of using to picket his horse, and with this he tied his pony to the neck of one of the antelope that he supposed was breathing its last, and proceeded on foot after the herd. He started on their trail, overtook them, and killed six; but when he returned, his pony was nowhere to be seen, and the antelope hitching-post was also missing. Starting in search of them, he found, to his surprise and amusement, the antelope leading the horse by the picket rope. He soon gave the animal its *coup de grace*, and, gathering up his spoils, he tied their heads together, two and two, and, throwing them across the horse, proceeded to the station driving his horse before him.

The little cavalcade must have presented an odd appearance as it entered Lakin; but, be this as it may, our friend gave the good towns-people a fine supply of antelope, and received excellent pay for them as well.

CHAPTER XIX.

A hunter's life is not always one of good luck, with plenty of game and big results, both as to meat and prices. On one occasion Youngblood started out to shoot over a range where usually there was game in abundance; but when he arrived at his destination, he found that the lakes had dried up, and the game had been forced to go elsewhere in search of water. He drove about for three days without firing a shot; for two of these days he was compelled to go entirely without food, and the pangs of hunger soon became excruciating. At last he struck a dog town, and by that time he was so famished that he could have chewed a pine board. He had never tasted a prairie-dog, and had not considered the animal as a viand

(233)

most worthy to tempt the appetite of an epicure; but this was no time to be dainty, so he turned his horses out, shot one of the little varmints, fried him nicely, and ate him. The food was so grateful to his empty stomach that he tried another, then another, and still another, until he had eaten six. It would be impossible for a man ordinarily to eat more than one; but our hunter was so hungry, and had absolutely nothing else in the way of food, that he easily got away with the half-dozen, and relished them, too.

After dinner he hitched up, and, after driving about forty miles, he fell in with a man named Edward Day, who had just killed a buffalo and had the humps with him. Youngblood told him that he was as hungry as a wolf, and wanted something to eat. Day was very hospitable, stopped, built a fire, and soon had an appetizing mess ready.

Youngblood asked his new friend where the game had gone to, and he replied that he had seen a large herd only about five miles from where they were then resting. This

news, with the buffalo humps, considerably
revived the jaded spirits of our hero, and he
at once started for the place indicated, and
killed six of the animals.

The next morning three men with a wagon
appeared at his improvised camp. They had
been out to kill buffalo, but had had no success, and were returning with heavy hearts.
After talking some time, they proposed to
Youngblood to give him $5 if he would show
them how to kill buffalo. The hunter had no
objection to making money so easily, and proceeded at once to give them the lesson. The
buffalo were very thick in that locality, and
there was no difficulty in finding all they
wanted. But the man who had made the
offer of $5 for the lesson was so much afraid
of the shaggy brutes that he could scarcely
be induced to go near enough to get his
money's worth. Youngblood, however, by
dint of ridicule and persuasion, got him as
close as he could, and showed him which one
to fire at, but his shot flew wide of the mark.
His teacher saw that he had a hard task

before him, and that he must get him nearer, so he himself shot and crippled one animal, and then started his pupil after it. The wounded buffalo moved off slowly, and the embryo hunter fired some twenty shots at it without the slightest visible effect. Finally, Youngblood brought him up within fifty yards, but by this time the poor fellow was so nervous that he was shaking as if he had an ague fit, and could not have hit a barn-door at five paces. The buffalo, seeing that it was about to be overtaken, turned and showed fight, and Youngblood was obliged to shoot it himself. He then told his companion to finish it quickly before it was dead, and the man ran up, and, after sending a ball into the buffalo's ham, turned and handed his instructor the $5. He was profuse in his thanks, and asked Youngblood to skin the head, declaring that he was going to have it stuffed, and when he was an old man he would exhibit it to his grandchildren as a relic of his exploits as a mighty hunter of the plains.

They then camped for the night, but when it came to building a fire with buffalo-chips, the strangers were too extremely nice to touch them, and Youngblood was obliged to gather all the fuel himself. It is no uncommon thing to find men who, on their first visit to the plains, are too dainty even to eat anything which has been cooked with this kind of fuel, but they soon conquer their squeamishness, take things as they find them, and " do in Rome as the Romans do."

About the only man that Youngblood ever knew to take kindly to buffalo-chips at the very first dash was an old friend of his—he sometimes rolls pills in Kansas—who had come out to take a look at the wild and woolly West, and while there he called on his old acquaintance. They went out together after antelope, and, stopping at the head of a small branch, found a pool of water at which, from the marks about it, it was evident that antelope had been drinking. They concluded to stop there and wait for the game to return; so they unhitched the horse, and drew the buggy down into a draw where it would be out of sight of the antelope, and then sat down to take a lunch. While they were eating, an antelope came in sight, within twenty paces of where they sat. Youngblood seized his gun, which happened to be within reach, and at the first shot brought down the animal. In a few moments two more came to the place where the dead one was lying, and he bagged both of them. He then told his friend to build a fire while he skinned the antelope, and they would have some fresh meat.

"All right," was the answer; "where can I find some wood?"

Youngblood pointed to a pile of "chips," and told him there was plenty of fuel.

To his surprise, and totally contrary to his expectations, the man jumped right into the midst of them, and, with no show of repugnance, began to rake them up with his hands, and a few minutes after was contentedly gnawing away at a chunk of bread in one hand and a lump of meat in the other.

CHAPTER XX.

Not long after the circumstances mentioned in the last chapter, Youngblood, in company with a friend, went south of the Arkansas River until they came to the North Fork, a distance of about thirty miles, and then traveled up this stream for another thirty miles, when they went south again to the Point of Rock, on the South Fork of Cimarron Creek. Here they came upon a large herd of buffalo, which Youngblood sent his friend to tackle, while he remained with the team. The buffalo tore down into a hollow, and, when they were fired upon, dashed straight toward the place where the wagon was. The team was a very wild one, and apt to run away at the slightest provocation, so Youngblood did not want to shoot; but as the buffalo whirled by at very close range,

(239)

his hunting instincts got the better of him, and he caught up his gun and blazed away. In his haste he forgot to draw the ramrod, which he had inserted in the gun, wrapped in oil tow, to prevent its rusting, and he shot stick and all, stringing two of the buffalo through the loins. The explosion startled the horses so that they were about to become unmanageable, and he was forced to rest content with this single shot, and give his whole attention to the team. When his friend came up he was surprised to see two dead buffalo, as he had heard only one shot, and the explanation simply increased his amazement.

They soon got the meat dressed and loaded, and began to retrace their way. After driving fifteen miles, they camped near a big spring for the night. About 9 o'clock they were startled from sleep by the howling of wolves, who, attracted by the smell of fresh meat, were prowling about the camp. There was a dog with them who bore no good-will to the beasts, and they finally came so

near that they and the dog kept up a continual racket. The dog would rush out at the wolves and chase them a short distance, when they would turn and drive him back, and then the whole performance would be gone over again. This continued, with brief intervals, throughout the whole night, and most effectually prevented Youngblood and his partner from obtaining a wink of sleep. The wolves were nearly starved, and seemed determined at all hazards to obtain something to eat.

At one time during the night it was really exciting and decidedly unpleasant for the two men. The wolves had chased the dog right up to where they were lying, when one of them attacked him. For some moments they fought viciously around, and even upon, the recumbent hunters, who had pulled the buffalo-robes well over them to protect them from injury, but who were anything but comfortable until the fight was over, and the dog had driven the wolf away. In the morning they rose, feeling much more

16

wearied than when they laid down. The
wolves were still all around them, and by
this time had grown quite friendly with the
dog, who was playing and frolicking with
them. There was very little profit to be
made by killing them, as wolf-skins brought
little or nothing in the market; but a few
well-directed shots scattered them, and
allowed the two friends, worn and weary, to
proceed to their destination.

CHAPTER XXI.

Our hero's next hunting expedition was
undertaken in company with an editor who
was anxious to see something of the big
game. The second night out they camped
on Carter Draw, on the banks of a large lake.
They had just begun their preparations for
breakfast, when they discovered that the
antelope in large numbers were coming to
the lake for water, and Youngblood told the
editor that if he would get breakfast, he, on
his side, would try to kill some of the
animals. He was very successful, returning,
after an hour's hunt, with ten of them. After
breakfast they gathered up the game, harnessed up, and drove to Syracuse Station,
about thirty miles distant, on the Atchison,

Topeka & Santa Fé Railroad. Here they shipped the antelope to Fisher, the hotel proprietor at Lakin.

From Syracuse they went about forty miles north, to a point near White Woman Creek, where they ran upon a herd of buffalo; but as it was sundown when they first saw them, Youngblood considered that it would be best to wait until morning before disturbing them. The herd was an enormous one, closely covering fully half a mile square, and the hunter and the editor retired to bed, full of joyous anticipations of the big load they would get in the morning; but, alack and alas! when the sun rose there was not a buffalo to be seen, high or low. The editor was loud in his expressions of disappointment; but the trail proved to be an easy one to follow, and, after fifteen miles travel, the herd was found lying down. Youngblood killed four of them, and the editor was satisfied.

They then drove to what is called the State Line Trail, and the hunter concluded to finish his load with antelope. When he had killed seven, a man with a team came along, and he hired him to take his load in to Sargeant Station, and thence ship it to Lakin.

With both wagon and hearts lightened, the partners traveled east a few miles, and halted on a small lake, a watering-place for both antelope and buffalo. During the night several of the former came down to the shore, and the editor shot one of them—his first, and, in all probability, his last, antelope. About 10 o'clock, the horses, which were picketed a short distance away, began to snort and exhibit evident signs of fright. Youngblood was on his feet in the twinkling of an eye, certain that the Indians were upon them; but soon saw, to his relief, that the cause of the horses' agitation was a herd of buffalo, only about fifty yards away, which had come down for water. Several of them were within a few feet of the camp, and they surrounded the wagon and so terrified one of the horses that he broke loose. It would have been an easy matter to have

killed several of them, but Youngblood did
not dare to shoot for fear of frightening the
horse still more and making him leave
entirely; so all he could do was to stand and
gaze at them until they had passed and he
could secure the horse again. His patience
was rewarded, however; for a few minutes
after he had the horse safely picketed, a
single buffalo came down to drink, and he
picked him off without the slightest difficulty. The two men then put on their clothes,
dressed the buffalo, and sat round the camp-
fire for the rest of the night. In the morning they drove five miles, and got six more
buffalo, which finished the load. When
these were dressed it was late in the afternoon, but as there was a moon that night,
Youngblood proposed to his partner to drive
into the station without further delay.
Shortly after they started, however, the
sky clouded over and it grew very dark, so
that Youngblood lost his bearings, and decided that it would be safer to proceed no
further.

When they went to picket their horses, however, they found, to their dismay, that they had left their picket-pins behind them in the place where they had camped the night before. There was only one thing to be done, and the two weary men were compelled to take turns in holding the horses until daylight showed them their whereabouts. Then they drove in to Aubery Station, sold what they could, and returned to Lakin. The proceeds of this hunt were seventeen antelope and eleven buffalo—not a bad showing, taking all the circumstances into consideration. The editor was highly delighted with his share in the expedition, and published an account of the trip in his paper.

At Lakin Youngblood found two sportsmen from Connecticut awaiting his return. They wanted to engage him simply as guide, as they desired to do all the shooting themselves. They possessed an armory of six guns—two breech-loading shotguns, two breech-loading rifles, and two eighteen-inch rifles. They agreed to pay the guide $3 a day from start to finish; and as soon as Young-blood was sufficiently rested, the party set forth and went about twenty miles south of the Arkansas River.

The particular pet of these sportsmen seemed to be the shotgun, and they wanted to go where there was an abundance of fowl to be had. It was something novel to the hunter of big game to see men who wished to go after ducks and snipes when there was plenty of buffalo and antelope to be had; but it was no affair of his—they were paying him; fowls they wanted, and fowls he found for them.

He conducted them, therefore, to a large lake which was literally alive with ducks and curlew. The curlew is about the size of the guinea-hen, and is most excellent eating, the flesh being delicate and finely flavored. There was also a kind of snipe about the size of a quail, and by no means to be despised by the epicure. With the innumerable quantities of duck, snipe, and curlew, the Connecticut men had the very finest sort of

sport of that particular kind that their souls delighted in. They seemed specially interested in the curlew, and regarded them as a great curiosity, with their long, slender legs, adapted for wading, and their curved beaks, about seven inches in length. These men were capital shots at small game. They would not shoot at a bird except when on the wing, and they never fired on a bunch of birds, but would make them fly up in the air, and then, selecting one, bring it down.

They kept up their sport for several days, until one of them, in firing at a duck on the wing, happened to shoot his comrade, who got within his range. Fortunately, the shot they were using was small bird-shot, so it did not seriously injure the man; but the accident put an end to the hunting, and sent the party back to Lakin.

Here Youngblood again found people waiting for him to pilot them out on a hunt. This time it was two doctors from Chicago, and as there was no bickering about terms, and our hunter felt fresh and entirely "fit," they started the next day. After traveling about twenty miles, they came to a lake where they stopped for the night. Here there were plenty of antelope, and they killed seven.

The doctors were provided with shotguns, and they kept blazing away at everything they saw. The wolves were decidedly obstreperous, and must have been very hungry, for they came prowling and howling very close to the camp, and the doctors killed several with their guns during the night.

They were well pleased with their sport; but, unlike the Connecticut men, they longed for the biggest of all game—a longing not uncharacteristic of the average Chicago man. So, in compliance with their desires, Youngblood harnessed up, the next morning, and they started out in search of buffalo. But, unfortunately, just at this time it seemed as if the whole world had gone mad on the subject of buffalo and antelope shooting. Some days one could see as many as fifty wagons going in all directions for meat; but by far the greater part of the would-be hunters would not have had the slightest idea what to do if they had happened, through good or evil fortune, to stumble upon a herd.

The fellows were around armed with anything they could lay their hands on—knives, pistols, axes, shotguns, etc. They would ask Youngblood in the most naive way if the buffalo would ever fight, and some of them seemed to imagine that they had nothing in the world to do except to amble calmly up to the side of one and put an end to its existence with pistol or knife, at their leisure. If they found a herd they would rush on, helter-skelter, as if they expected the animals to stand still to be caught by their tails and have their throats cut.

In fact, the crazy rush and racket of these greenhorns frightened the buffalo and antelope quite out of that portion of the country, and caused them to seek a refuge from the din and noise further west, whence they did not return for over six months, frightened out of their senses as they were.

Most of these raw hunters were men who had been gulled by land agents into coming West, the hope held out to them being cheap lands, a hope destined never to be realized.

At all events, they had effectually driven away the buffalo, and Youngblood had to take his Chicago doctors back with their longings for big game unrealized.

CHAPTER XXII.

We shall devote this chapter to three hunts which our hero was concerned in in the seventies, and which possess certain points of interest; but before relating them it may be well to give here a brief description of Western Kansas in general, and its rivers and river valleys in particular.

Beginning at the northwest corner of the State and coming south, the first stream is the Republican River, which has its source in Colorado, near the foot of the mountains, is fed by springs, and when it runs into Kansas is about 180 feet wide. The Republican River has several southern tributaries, many of which are broad streams and skirted with some timber, though not enough to make them good places for the location of saw-mills. The next river of note, as you go south, is the Solomon River, which in the extreme western portion of the State is shallow and narrow; but, further on, it receives the waters of many large springs, and becomes quite a stream. In places there is considerable timber upon its banks, and all through this valley there are many capital sites for a ranch. South of Solomon River is Goose Creek, fed by springs, and with some timber; in many places there is good meadow land. The next stream south is South Smoky River, broad and deep, with more or less wooded banks, making an excellent place for ranches; but most of the land is already taken up.

South of the Arkansas River, the country is well wooded and watered, and there are many valleys suitable for ranchers to settle in. All the valley of the Arkansas River, with its abundant streams and good grazing, is the best buffalo region on the face of the globe.

Although Youngblood's buffalo-hunting has by no means been confined exclusively to Kansas, as he has frequently gone into Nebraska, Colorado, New Mexico, Indian Territory, and Texas, there is hardly a square mile of Western Kansas and its contiguous territory that he has not explored. There is not a creek that he can not describe; not a bit of timber that he has not seen, nor a range of hills with which he is not familiar; in fact, he is probably more intimately acquainted with that country than any other living man.

But as to the hunts that we spoke of at the beginning of the chapter. The first one was undertaken with a man named Edward Riley, and the point of departure was Wallace Station, on the Kansas Pacific Railroad. On the second day out a large herd was found; they were coming directly toward the hunters, and, as the prairie was on fire, they were in a general stampede. Youngblood left Riley with the team, and killed five in a very short space of time; but it was not long before the fire was right upon them, at which Riley became so frightened that he utterly lost his head, and while Youngblood's attention was directed toward something else, he turned the team and drove off at a gallop, thinking only of making his own escape, and leaving his companion alone to manage the best way he could. After he had gone a short distance, however, he recovered his senses, and turned to come back; but by this time the smoke was so dense that he could see nothing of Youngblood. The latter went on, meanwhile, and dressed the buffalo he had killed. There was really no danger from the fire where he was, as they had taken the precaution to clear a large space. After his work was done he waited patiently until dark; but his runaway partner not appearing, he began to cast about to see how he was going to keep from freezing. The weather was growing very cold, and he was in his shirt-sleeves, for he had, unluckily, left his coat in the wagon when he started after the buffalo,

and, of course, Riley had driven off with it.
What to do our shivering hunter scarcely
knew; but he finally took the hides of two
of the buffalo he had killed and rolled himself up in them as tight as he could. It
was not long before the hides froze and
became as solid as a plaster mold. There
was plenty of warmth in this covering, but
the enclosed figure could not move an inch.
He made the best of it, however, and lay thus
enwrapped until morning, when, by dint of
hard squeezing and struggling, he managed
to crawl out of his narrow cell. His first
thought was to find out what had become of
his partner, and he mounted a high hill
where a good view could be obtained in all
directions; but no trace of Riley was to be
seen. Late in the evening, however, the
truant hove in sight, and, in spite of all,
Youngblood was glad enough to see him;
for, as he had no matches to start a fire to
cook anything, he had not had an atom to
eat since they parted, twenty-four hours
before. After the pangs of hunger were sat-
17

isfied, they loaded up their meat and started for Goose Creek; but in a very short time the skies grew dark and lowering, and there were even indications of a snow-storm. They did not go far, therefore, but drew up their wagon and camped in a draw. In the morning they had to dig themselves out, for the snow had drifted round their tent to a height of four feet, although it was not more than six inches deep on a level. They tried to proceed on their journey, but it was still snowing, and so cold and disagreeable that they had to stop again, and in a very short time found themselves snow-bound. When it at last cleared off, and they began to make preparations to move out, they found their wagon so badly snowed in that it was a long and difficult task to shovel it out. After a hard tug, they finally reached Wallace, just two weeks from the time they started.

When they drove into the station, the people came running excitedly in all directions to ask if they had seen or heard any-

thing of the Indians. It seems that there had
been a big fight in the vicinity of the station
—a fight in which twenty-eight Indians had
been killed—and the inhabitants had given
Youngblood and his companion up for lost,
although they, in their blissful ignorance,
had never dreamed of danger from the red-
skins.

Shortly after this buffalo hunt, Youngblood was engaged in a wild-horse chase.
Three of them started out to take three
herds—one apiece—and with them were four
hands to help. On the second day our
hero killed a load of buffalo, and dispatched
a man to Lakin with it. They then kept on
until they found the wild horses, when they
camped and prepared for business.

Youngblood selected for his a herd of
twenty-six—twenty-five bays and a roan—
while the other two took, one a herd of
twenty-two, and the other a herd of twenty-
four. They were all three on their mettle,
and each determined to outstrip his companions. The herds started in the same general

direction, going northwest into Colorado, about 100 miles from the place they were first discovered. They first passed through a very dry country, but finally came to a belt of land where the rains had been plentiful, and the grass was good. The horses wanted to stay here, and began circling about. After fifteen days hard driving, the three men finally reached Lakin with fifty-six head.

Here had been prepared a corral, made of railroad ties set about eighteen inches in the ground, and with two wings built in the same way. It was with no little difficulty that all the horses were driven into the corral, and, even when this was successfully accomplished, there was a still harder job on hand; for all the captives had to be broken. The method used was this: An experienced cowboy throws a lasso over the head of one of the horses and chokes him down, when he is bridled and held prostrate by long ropes until he is conquered and consents to be led about. It is important that this breaking-in process be undertaken as soon as the horses are penned, and before they have time to rest; and they must be handled every day afterward until they become perfectly tame and docile.

The third hunt that Youngblood made about this time was after buffalo. He started out from Aubrey, and proceeded north of the Arkansas River. When he had driven about forty miles he came to a small lake where there were evident signs of a recent visit from some of the desired game.

Youngblood soon found the direction in which their trail led, and followed it up. When he had gone about five miles he discovered a herd, and, leaving his two men with the wagons, he crept up as close as he could; but, in spite of his best efforts, he succeeded in wounding only one before they dashed over a hill and were out of sight. He noticed, however, that the herd was bearing round the hill, and he ran across to intercept them if possible. Suddenly, as he was running along at full speed, he heard something behind, and, turning, saw a buffalo-calf galloping after him. It had probably been asleep when the rest of the herd had been started. It was a small one, and as the hunter stopped it came straight up to him, only to be seized and held until the men and teams came up, when it was tied and put into a wagon.

Youngblood then continued his way round the hill, and when he got to the other side he found that the buffalo he had wounded had dropped down in the road; but, to his unbounded surprise, one of its hams had entirely disappeared. This, however, was soon explained, for on looking up the road he saw a wagon with three men in it driving rapidly away. The thieves paid dearly for their knavery, however, for lying near the buffalo was a fine field-glass which they had dropped in their haste, and which Youngblood appropriated, considering himself well paid for his ham. The next morning, having camped only a mile away, he saw two of the fellows riding back and forth, in all probability searching for the glass, which they never found.

That day our hunter drove a few miles and found five buffalo, but only got one when it began to rain, and he was obliged to return to the station. The calf died on the journey. Despite his rather poor luck with buffalo, Youngblood managed to kill enough antelope to make out a load, and to feel well repaid for his time.

CHAPTER XXIII.

WISE MEN OF THE EAST—AN AUTHORITY ON WOODCHUCK—BOUND TO EAT IT, MUD-HEN OR NOT—THE TALE OF A TAIL.

During the summer of 1877, Youngblood did but little hunting, as pelts and skins are of small value during warm weather, and he did not care to kill the goose which had thus far supplied him with golden—or rather paper—dollars.

However, he kept his eye in training and his trigger-finger limbered up by piloting a great many parties, tenderfooted and otherwise, out on the prairies, and he did not realize until then the close resemblance that existed between a coyote and a jack-rabbit; at least, those two quadrupeds appeared to look so much alike in the eyes of the wise men of the East that one really couldn't tell what these Nimrods had brought down until the last man of their party had given his opinion and backed it up by copious references to Buffon and a few illustrated posters supplied by that great educator of the youth of this country—Mr. P. T. Barnum.

Among those for whom our hero acted in this capacity was a party of surveyors who were laying out a route for a branch of the Rock Island Railroad, and who wished him to accompany them for the double purpose of keeping the wolf from the door and supplying them with fresh meat. It was rather fortunate that he was with the party, for the young man in charge of the commissary department apparently did not know the difference between a sage-hen and a prairie-chicken, or at least thought that, in the absence of the latter, the former would fill in a satisfactory manner the empty pot that usually hung on their camp-fire, and that empty void which nature particularly abhors. To one who has attempted to eat sage-hens, it will be unnecessary to say that one application is enough, and that the game Youngblood was able to furnish made a most desirable change, as even customers of Delmonico's will admit that brook-trout, prairie-chicken, teal-duck, antelope, and now and then a tender bear-steak, are rather better than the young surveyor's sage-hen and Chicago sour-bellies.

As soon as the weather grew cooler, Young-blood returned to headquarters, and in the month of October, while preparing to make a *real* hunt, was prevailed upon by an old friend of his, named Bennett, to take him and a Mr. Weeks, of Iowa, for a little tour.

Hank Bennett had seen our hero come in from many a hunt, and was wild to get a crack at some game himself; while Weeks had probably never seen anything wild larger than an Iowa gopher, or perhaps a woodchuck of the crop of 1840. Young-blood was quite willing to give them a good time; so he loaded up his prairie-schooner, and they started, the objective point being a stream about twenty-five miles distant.

Here they camped, and while Hank was getting things in shape for supper, Youngblood tried a new Winchester on a few jack-rabbits; but as they had plenty of meat with them, he did not bother to get them, although he wished afterward that he had not left them lying round.

After they had eaten, smoked their pipes, and swapped the customary number of stories over the camp-fire, they turned in with the expectation of a good sleep and an early start; but were fooled, as far as sleep was concerned, for the jack-rabbits Young-blood had killed brought the coyotes and wolves around in hundreds, and their snarling and fighting kept up so that rest was out of the question.

The brutes finally settled around a couple of the rabbits, and were holding a regular town-meeting; so Youngblood, in despair, got up, and, taking a piece of burning wood from the fire, gave them a lively chase, which put an end to their yelling for the night.

The party got a good start in the morning, and pushed on for a pool about twenty miles distant, where Youngblood proposed to make their permanent camp. Prairie-dogs were thicker than vermin on a Sioux's back, and Weeks said that he had never seen so many young woodchucks before, so took advantage of the opportunity and caught two, declaring he wanted to bring them up as pets. It is to be hoped that they have grown to the size of the regulation Iowa woodchuck by this time; Weeks said they would, and he appeared to be an authority on woodchucks.

About 4 o'clock in the afternoon the pool was reached, and while Youngblood and Weeks were unhitching, Hank Bennett started off on a tour of observation. In about ten minutes he came running back, with his long, yellow hair flying, and his thin legs going too fast to cast a shadow, with the information that a little further up the pool was filled with ducks, and that he wanted to have a show at them.

He was very much excited, and Youngblood said "Go ahead!" so he made a break for the wagon to get his gun, but was so torn up with the thought of ducks that he carried one of the "medicine" jugs about five rods from the schooner before Youngblood informed him that it contained bait for fishing, and could not be used to good advantage on duck. He seemed surprised, and said he thought "everything went" while hunting, but finally got out his gun, and Weeks went with him to bring in the dead.

Youngblood heard a good many shots shortly after, and in about half an hour back came the boys with the game. Hank had five birds, and it was hard to tell who felt the prouder, Bennett for killing them, or Weeks for being in such good company.

When they got within speaking distance, Hank held up the game and called out:

"Ain't they dandies?"

"What?" asked Youngblood.

"Why, these teal, of course."

Youngblood could scarcely repress his laughter. "Teal!" he chuckled. "Why, you hayseed, those are mud-hens, and a starved coyote would twist up his tail in pain if he was asked to eat them."

Poor Hank felt very sore over this, but admitted that his friend was right, after he had tried to eat one of the hens which he roasted for his supper. The same old hen, with Bennett's tooth-marks in it, is probably there yet, for there never yet was found anybody or anything that could eat one.

The next morning, while Youngblood was smoking his pipe and taking things easy, Bennett came rushing up and told him that there was an antelope a little way from camp, and wanted him to go and get it. It is needless to say the hunter was willing, and, getting his rifle, he started, with Hank and Weeks trailing after, they wishing to see the operation from start to finish.

The game was a single buck, and was feeding quietly in an open spot, so that it was necessary to use great caution in getting within range. This was rather a difficult matter for Youngblood to accomplish, with the boys tramping on his trail; but, after a good deal of crawling and skirmishing, he got the drop on Mr. Buck, who threw up his hands, or rather his tail, and passed in his checks, much to the delight of Weeks and Bennett, who then voted the "hunt" a big success, and were ready to go home, thinking that the combination had done wonders.

This proposition was agreeable to Youngblood, so they headed for Coolidge, and, after traveling eight or ten miles, antelope were discovered some distance to the left. Leaving Weeks and Bennett with the team, which by that time had been backed into a hollow out of sight, Youngblood started for the game, going around them for the purpose of driving them toward the wagon when they should break away after his fire. They were grazing toward the spot where he had left his outfit, and when within seventy-five or one hundred yards of it, he fired, bringing down a fine buck and wounding another. The latter made straight for the wagon, but it was evident from his jumps that he was badly hurt.

Of course, Youngblood started after him at a lively gait, and was just going to pump

another dose of lead into him, when who should jump from a hole close to him but Hank, who made a dash at the antelope, and in some way got hold of his stump of a tail, and held on like grim death to a dead nigger. The buck·kept going, however, almost jerking Hank's teeth out at every spring, and making his legs look like wagon-spokes going at a "forty" pace; but the harder he jumped, the madder got Bennett, and the stronger got his hold.

"Go it!" yelled Hank. "Go it, you darned old white-bellied goat! I'm from Posey County, Indiana, and you can't shake me!"

But the louder Bennett yelled, the more scared the buck got, and put in his best licks for freedom, clearing from ten to fifteen feet at a jump.

Hank began to think he had bitten off a bigger cud than he could chew, and began to scream:

"Charley! Weeks! Here, you; somebody head us darned fools off!"

18

But suddenly, while the other two were paralyzed with laughter, the buck stepped into a dog-hole and fell, and Hank made a jump for his head, and sat on it until Youngblood ran up and cut his throat.

Bennett was very proud of his achievement, and wanted to start right then for Coolidge and tell his wife all about the trip; but night was coming on, and, as they were fifteen or twenty miles from town, his companions prevailed upon him to give up the idea of walking in, that night; so, after supper, they all turned in, got a good sleep, and started early the next morning for Coolidge.

During the ride in, Youngblood added five antelope to the lot, while Weeks and Bennett knocked out several jack-rabbits and ducks; which ended what was, for a short trip, one of the pleasantest picnics our hero ever attended, and equally enjoyed by all.

CHAPTER XXIV.

In the latter part of October, Youngblood and one of his sons made elaborate preparations for an extended hunt, and on about the 20th of the month started, with two teams, for "No Man's Land," where they expected to find buffalo, antelope, etc., in abundance. Their route took them through Minneapolis County, and at every stopping-place they were objects of much interest to the inhabitants of the towns, who gathered round the wagons with that intense interest which anything out of the common run excites in the minds of people who have more time to devote to other persons' affairs than they can possibly spare for their own. The settlers were much astonished at the large quantity of ammunition carried, and

seemed to think that immediate efforts were
to be made to exterminate all the red-skins
west of the Rockies. Some of the more in-
quisitive began to handle the poison, and to
speculate as to what use it was to be put to,
and were greatly delighted when a smart
Aleck informed them that they were hired by
the Government to settle the vexed question
of Mr. "Lo" in this manner, they believ-
ing, with gallant Phil. Sheridan, that the
only truly good Indian is a dead one. After
this shrewd guess had been made, and good
luck wished them, together with the assurance that the hunters "knew their business," they pushed on to the southern line
of the State of Colorado, where their business again demanded the attention of the
guessers, and caused plenty of money to
go over the bar at the "Little Heaven"
saloon.

Cimarron River was soon reached, where
the party was delayed a day or two by a
threatened storm, which fortunately did not
materialize; but, as game was very scarce in

that section, another jump of fifty miles was
made, to where there was a good outlook for
what the expedition was after. Enough
antelope, rabbits, etc., were killed to keep
the larder well filled with fresh meat, and
while finishing a dinner from this bill of fare,
one day, a party of typical cowboys came
dashing up on their ratty-looking cayuses,
and, after giving the customary yells, and
shots from their "44s," the "boss" said:
"Youngblood, have you got any fresh meat?
We ain't proud; the last stuff of that kind
I eat was the left ear of a Government mule;
so if you can take that taste out of my
mouth, I'll give you the first two-headed
bull-calf that my bronco drops."

Of course, in that part of the country
everything is fun, and a man is expected
to take anything he wants, except horses—
those the line is drawn at. But when a fellow has certain reasons for wishing for
another man's life, he may have it, if he can
get the drop first, and no questions are asked.

The "boss" of this particular gang was

"Cheyenne Jim," who had the reputation of being a pretty good man at any kind of gun game; so, after the "punchers" had filled up on antelope and such truck, they began fooling with their "44s," and did some shooting that would make Doctor Carver's hair curl tighter than the eastern barbers are able to make it.

Jim had downed his gang in shooting at a mark, and began to banter Youngblood (who had up to that time taken no part in the fun) to shoot against him. The latter held off for some time; but Jim was so dead-set to have a "go" that he even offered to bet his new "slickers" against Youngblood's hat that he could beat him. Now, the "slickers" were new, and would just about fit Youngblood, so it didn't take long to get him warmed up. The rest of the cow-propellers gathered round, and yelled like wild men when Jim drove a hole through the spot in the ace of spades which was stuck up on a tree about fifty yards distant, and hit the card with his two remaining shots.

Youngblood didn't say much, but put up another ace on the same tree, and fired three times in as many seconds. When he dropped his revolver, the pip was out of the ace, but no marks of the two other bullets, and the cowboys raised a great noise, feeling certain that Jim had won.

"Hold on," says Youngblood; "those are pretty good 'schaps' you're wearing, Jim, and I'll bet you my gun against them that I beat you."

Jim couldn't take the bet too quick, and the gang went to the tree to decide the wager. Sure enough, the center-spot was gone from Jim's card, which also showed two other holes within two inches of the first one. In Youngblood's card there was only one mark, right in the exact center; but without changing a muscle of his face, he pulled out his knife and showed Mr. Cheyenne Jim that all three of his bullets had gone in the single hole!

There was nothing for Jim to do but shed his "slickers" and "schaps," and admit defeat, which he did gracefully, and, with a sorrowful and sickly smile on his face, "cinched" up, and, with his gang, rode off, taking with him a pot of bear's grease presented by Youngblood, who knew that in the absence of "slickers" he would have to apply it next morning, or do his eating standing up.

By the time this monkey-business was over, it was too late to think of doing any work; so after supper the hunters turned in, to wake the next morning and find two of the horses missing.

Now, to be a couple of hundred miles or so away from home, without horses, and with Indians liable to turn up at any minute, is not a pleasant sensation; so the first thing to do was to get the live stock.

At first the thought was that the cowboys had taken them as a practical joke; but Youngblood soon found their trail, which was very fresh, so concluded they had strayed off only, and sent his son to round them up, while he looked after the balance of the outfit.

The younger man had not been gone long when Youngblood caught sight of two antelope about 1,000 yards off, and, getting his gun, started for them. The only thing that could hide him from their sight was a patch of sage-brush here and there, and, after a good deal of crawling, he finally got within 500 yards, and let go; the buck dropped dead in his tracks, and as the doe started for the timber, another shot made her change her mind, and she went to join her mate.

In about half an hour the horses were driven back to the wagons and hitched up to get the two dead antelope. When they were reached, Youngblood was surprised to find them already half eaten, and to see three gray wolves, about as big as a good-sized Newfoundland dog, sneaking off into the timber, and licking their chops as though they enjoyed the joke they had played on him.

This was a little too much for an old hunter to stand; so, after staying in the neighborhood for a few days, and getting about twenty more head of antelope (about all that remained of the herd), Youngblood started his son for Boston, Col., while he remained to have *his* fun with the wolves. Making a fresh-meat drag of a couple of the dead antelope, he hauled them in a circle of about two miles, to give a strong scent, and then returned to within fifty yards of his starting-point.

By this time the sun was only about half an hour high, and the gray boys were beginning to gather at the scent, so the poison-boxes were brought into use, and a toothsome repast prepared for the expected dear ones. Youngblood didn't care to trouble himself to act as host, knowing that his guests did not stand upon the ceremony of host, so he turned in to await the result of his feast.

In the morning he counted thirty-six heretofore able-bodied wolves who had become tired of life, and taking their clothes—they having no further use for them—he left their bodies to the tender mercies of their brethren, who, with that generosity peculiar to their race, cleaned them up in short order.

Pulling up stakes, our hero started for Boston to pick up his son, getting on the way in the neighborhood of fifty antelope, and then passed through Minneapolis, Col., and Border City, Kan., toward Coolidge, where he intended to dispose of the skins and pelts taken.

When a day or two out from the latter point, he gathered in twelve antelope, which were taken into town and sold to Messrs. Hawkins & Crittenden, butchers, who were mighty glad to get them.

On the whole, the trip was a good one, as it ended profitably, and without the hardships and dangers which attended other expeditions made by Youngblood, both before and after.

CHAPTER XXV.

TERRIBLE WEATHER—PRAIRIE HOSPITALITY
—A GAME OF BLUFF—YOUNGBLOOD TO
THE FORE.

After spending a few days to give their
stock a little rest and lay in the necessary
supplies for another trip, Youngblood and
his son again started out "on business;"
but came nearer reaching the "happy hunting-ground" of Indian tradition than (for
them) the more satisfactory stamping-place
of the buffalo and the antelope. The first
night out, one of their horses was taken
sick in some mysterious manner, and died,
leaving them, at the outset of their journey,
in a position much like a rudderless ship in
mid ocean.

The sudden taking off of this animal was,
to say the least, suspicious; and as the success of our friends in the hunting-field had
caused considerable envy to be felt by less

fortunate sportsmen, Youngblood naturally suspected foul play; but, nothing daunted by their serious mishap, they gave no thought to abandoning their trip, and the younger hunter was dispatched to civilization for a new horse. Immediately upon his return they again got under way, pointing for the "Neutral Ground," and in about six days began to strike antelope in great plenty.

We will not tire our readers with a description of their various devices for securing these wary animals; suffice it to say that they soon obtained their load, and started on their return journey for the purpose of disposing of the results of their unerring rifles.

The weather by this time had become exceedingly cold, and at each settlement which they passed through stories were told of the horrible deaths by freezing that befell the unfortunates who became lost on the prairies. To those who have never experienced really cold weather on the plains, imagination is but a small aid to the realizing sense which we each possess, and no description can adequately describe the feeling that comes over one who is alone in a trackless waste of snow, with nothing human within sight or hearing. The clear, dry air almost freezes the marrow in one's bones, bringing in its still embrace a sensation of almost pleasure, which to submit to is death.

At Boston and Minneapolis, Col., as well as at Border City, Kan., Youngblood and his son heard continual reports of deaths from the terrible weather, and were urged to wait for a favorable change, but declined doing so, heroically pushing on over ground covered with snow to the depth of from three to four feet on a level.

Finally, however, home was reached, and the tired men were heartily welcomed by their friends, the jaded beasts also coming in for their share in the general rejoicing.

After resting for a month, Youngblood became tired of what to his active disposition seemed idleness, and made up his mind to take a run into "No Man's Land," to see what could be found in the way of game.

For about four days his journey was an uneventful one; but one night, when he was near the center of the "Panhandle" strip, a fierce hail-storm came up, nearly freezing him to death, he being obliged to make his bed in four inches of hail, and on wet blankets. The night seemed endless; he dared not sleep, knowing that if he did so he would never awake, and when morning dawned he was nearly overcome with fatigue and cold, and having no fuel, of course, a fire was impossible. The hail, however, soon disappeared, and he finally was able to make a fire, fortunately having some matches which he had wrapped in a piece of rubber cloth, thus keeping them dry. These storms usually cover a long but narrow section of country, Youngblood finding the one in question to be about three miles wide, and our readers may feel certain that he was glad when he was out of the "belt," and

seated before a huge fire of buffalo-chips for
a thorough warming.

After this agreeable pastime had been
indulged in to his satisfaction, and the crav-
ings of the inner man appeased, he again
started.   After traveling about thirty miles
he reached a spring, where he found two
men in camp.   With that hospitality that is
customary in the West, they invited him to
spend the night, an invitation which he
gladly accepted; and the result was that a
very pleasant day was passed with them—a
sudden snow-storm making still closer the
intimacy which is usually the result of three
in a bed—or rather three in a tent.

With clearing weather our hero bade good-
by to his newly made friends, and started
for a small stream some twenty miles south.
Here he found two men who had evidently—
in their minds—preëmpted the hunting priv-
ileges about it, as they had "bluffed out"
other hunters as fast as they came.   They
began to operate on Youngblood in the same
manner; but he was too old a bird to be so

19

easily caught, and after apparently swallow-
ing their tales of Mexican Rangers coming
up and arresting men almost without number, and taking them off for trial, he finally
began to laugh, and said: "Well, boys,
that's a pretty good tune; but I have been
listening to that kind of singing for eighteen
years, so don't get discouraged if I don't get
enthusiastic and say it's original music."

This appeared to surprise the would-be
owners of the earth, and they asked if he
really had been about there so long.

"Why," said our wily old friend, "I guess
that's a fact, for I helped clear the wolves
out of this country; but I see there are two
that I kinder overlooked. I'm still after
'em, though."

The men saw the point, and were so much
pleased with the hearty way of the sturdy
hunter that they became very friendly, and
the result was that he remained several days
with them.

There were a good many antelope—about
twenty-six in all—in the region, which soon

fell victims to his faithful Winchester, and a couple of buffalo also "bit the dust" at his fire.

A Mr. French, from Maine, was one of the men just referred to, and he and Youngblood soon became very "chummy." This gentleman was a Mason and a fine fellow, in every way worthy to be associated with our hero.

No more game appearing inclined to turn up, a move toward Coolidge, Kan., was made, where, upon arrival, Youngblood found one of his sons very sick, with Doctors Smith and Boggs in attendance, who, although doing all in their power, had given him up as beyond hope. This was truly a sad home-coming for our gallant friend; but his grief was soon turned to joy, for, through the great care of these able physicians, and aided by the best gift of a stalwart father to his son—a glorious constitution—the disease turned, and happiness was soon in full command at the hunter's western home.

CHAPTER XXVI.

On the 10th of March, although it was still unusually cold, Youngblood and French started again for "No Man's Land," being determined to work it for all it was worth in the way of game; and after traveling four days, reached the center of the strip. Just before they arrived at this point, they discovered a gray wolf on their trail, and as our friend has the same affection for wolves as we are informed His Satanic Majesty holds for holy water, he left the team, telling French to drive on, and in a few minutes returned with a skin which looked suspiciously like that worn by Mr. Wolf, and if the latter ever reached the bosom of his family, he must have made the journey without a pelt!

A tremor of interest was also caused by the discovery of some animals quite a dis-

tance from them, and after using all the
tricks of old hunters, finally our adventurers
drew near enough to discover that they were
cattle and a bunch of wild horses which had
come in for water. It was natural to suppose that buffalo would also make use of
the spring, and therefore Youngblood and
French kept watch during the night, "laying for them;" but they were too cunning,
and failed to appear.

It being useless to remain in this spot any
longer, a start was made toward the south,
and after going about twenty-five miles they
reached a spring where three men were found
who had been on a hunt, and had bagged
one buffalo. This showed that there were
some in the neighborhood, and a wait over
night was made, but as no game appeared,
our party bore off to the east twenty miles,
reaching Howard's ranch in time to avoid a
two-days' snow-storm. French concluded
that the work was too tough for even him,
and consequently Youngblood, who wouldn't
be "bluffed" by any one, started south

alone, reaching Rollins' ranch, which was situated on a fine stream.

Rollins, who proved to be a fine fellow, was at home, and he and Youngblood soon became very great friends. The former insisted upon the latter's putting in a few days with him, and Youngblood was nothing loath to do so, as Rollins said buffalo came to the stream daily for water. The house was beautifully situated, and commanded a fine view of as delightful a scene as is often witnessed; the rolling prairie extending in one direction as far as the eye could see, while there was a fine belt of timber to the right, the wood extending down the stream for a considerable distance, and one sitting in the door of the cabin could see the pool frequented by the big brutes our friend was after.

Youngblood was sitting about, smoking, occasionally glancing out for game, while Rollins was preparing a dinner which a lover of game would go miles to partake of. The delicious aroma of venison and brook-trout was playing about Youngblood's nostrils, when, glancing out of the door, he saw a fine buffalo-bull leave the water, and after shaking his shaggy head, as it would seem, by way of challenge, started away. When discovered, the bull was about half a mile off; but Youngblood sprang for his rifle, and in an instant was out of the door and after him like a deer. The immense brute passed over a ridge before our hunter had gotten within range; but he ran to the top of the hill, and, although the shot was a long one, he fired, wounding the brute, who at once turned, and started round the base of the eminence. But the monarch of the plains was not to get off so easily, as he had met his master this time. Youngblood, anticipating his actions, ran to the foot of the hill to await his coming, and had hardly got into position when the infuriated bull charged him, and would have put an end to these adventures had not a perfectly aimed shot brought him to his knees, and the gleaming knife of our hunter sent him to the land of the good buffalo.

While Youngblood was returning to the ranch, he met Rollins coming from there with two knives in his hand.   .

"What are those for?" asked Youngblood.

"Why," said Rollins, "to undress Mr. Buffalo, of course; you didn't think I wanted to eat him with his coat on, did you?"

"You're fooled this time," said our hunter, by way of a joke; "I missed him."

"Come off!" remarked the ranch-owner. "I'd hate to have to eat all you didn't miss. You don't miss nothing. Where's the bull?"

Youngblood's joke would not go down in the face of his reputation, so he finally admitted that he had not missed this time; and the buffalo was soon stripped of his hide and taken to the ranch, where some juicy steaks were served for supper, much to the surprise of some travelers who drove up just before dusk, as they had no idea that such game was within a hundred miles of the house.

It was a jolly party that spent that night

at Rollins' ranch, and those present will not soon forget the good cheer that was freely offered by their host. The party consisted of Dr. I. J. Nair, Messrs. J. H. Becker, J. W. Whitesell, and Daniel Crough, besides Youngblood and Rollins. The first-named gentlemen were out for the purpose of selecting a town-site, and had located it a few miles from Rollins', being much pleased with the surrounding country, where, before many years have passed, will be found one of the most prosperous cities in the West, as nature has abundantly supplied it with her choicest gifts, and these gentlemen certainly are brainy enough to do the rest.

Of course, many a story was told that night round the open fire, each being obliged to contribute his share to the merriment. Doctor Nair (who is now working emigration for the "buffalo pastures") gave some vivid stories of his experience during the war; while Youngblood was obliged to open his pack, and, in his modest way, told hunting stories that would cause one to look nervously toward the door at one moment, while the next, his hearers wished for day, that they also might try the fascination of the chase.

But the best of friends must part, and the sun rises with unpleasant regularity; so, in the course of time, it was necessary to stop the fun and give some attention to the morrow. Consequently, after a few more pulls at their pipes, the company turned in, and when day broke, the next morning, it was "up and away" with the irrepressible Youngblood, who turned his refreshed horses toward the river or stream Alfreo, which was about eighty miles distant. Upon his arrival, he found two men encamped, and remained with them several days, during which time his deadly rifle was brought into use, and, as a result, several antelope were added to his store, and two buffalo paid that tribute which their race seems to owe him.

On the whole, however, "the game was hardly worth the candle," as the French king puts it, and after waiting at this point a few days longer, our hunter concluded to run home for repairs and ammunition; and therefore turned his horses' heads toward Coolidge, disposing of his load at good prices at Boston and Minneapolis, and reaching his destination in good order, to find all well, and with another batch of stories for the youngsters, who will, perhaps, in days to come, follow his example.

CHAPTER XXVII.

NO PAY, NO MEAT—ON THE TRAIL AGAIN— WATER, WATER EVERYWHERE!

The growing scarcity of buffalo in his immediate neighborhood prompted Young-blood, in April, 1878, to plan a more extended trip, and, when all was ready, he started, with one of his boys, for a point some 200 miles south of Coolidge. The main object of their journey was to capture buffalo-calves, but they prepared for anything from the monarch of the plains to a Chicago "bunko-steerer;" but, of course, the latter were hardly to be expected. On the second day out, a couple of antelope were discovered feeding a short distance from the road; these they killed, and their carcasses were thrown on the wagon, which went creaking along until a house was reached, some ten miles further on. Upon hearing the noise made by the team, the

owner of the cabin came to the door. In
personal appearance, this individual much
resembled a Georgia "Cracker," and he
looked so hungry that Youngblood said:

"Want these antelope?"

"Yes, stranger, you bet!"

"You can buy them cheap."

"Buy! I ain't buying till I sell my hoop-
poles."

"Well, can't trade, then; bye, bye!"

And away creaked the wagon, little knowing how it would be called upon to groan
later, for sand-hills were soon reached, and
the ten miles through which that devoted
vehicle passed would have tamed the proud
spirit of the most arrogant "Tally-Ho"
coach in existence.

In the sage-brush which dotted these
hills were innumerable prairie-chickens—or
rather hens, as age should command respect
at all times—and the junior Youngblood
was anxious to get some for the evening
meal. This he did, but as the birds were of
the "vintage of '38," that regard for antiq-

uities which is part of the make-up of the true hunter would not permit them to be eaten. They were *tasted*, and that was quite enough; the pork-barrel contained delicacies compared to them.

Passing through "No Man's Land," our travelers finally reached the "Panhandle" of Texas, where they found John Rawlins' ranch, on the banks of a stream called Cold-water. On learning of the object of their journey, Rawlins said that he had cows for the calves, and wanted to join our friends in their search. This was quite agreeable to Youngblood; consequently, after refilling the water-kegs (the country being very dry), the reinforced army took up its march for the diminutive bison.

After two days' traveling, a section of the country was struck which was as devoid of vegetation as though a fire had swept over it, and, in looking for a grazing spot for the live stock, they finally found a depression covered with grass, and which had evidently been the bed of a small lake, and just the

camping-ground wanted. After congratulating themselves on having their necessities so
easily supplied, supper was eaten, the horses
and mules picketed, and the human part of
the outfit made up their shake-downs in the
body of the wagon for a comfortable night,
and dreams of buffalo-calves galore. But,
while man proposes, others get their work
in; and about 10 o'clock it began to cloud
up, with lightning playing across the heavens most vividly. Then it began to rain;
first came "the gentle dew" that Shakes-
peare speaks of, and then St. Swithin took
his hand in the game, and how it did hail!
This picturesque but uncomfortable mass
nearly filled the body of the wagon, and, to
add to the discomfort of the night, it suddenly changed to rain, making a mixture to
be carefully avoided,

Nearly chilled to death, our unfortunates
waited for the next change, fondly hoping
that whatever might come would be warm;
when Rawlins' horse began to snort, plunge,
and kick in the most outrageous manner.

Youngblood was anxious to learn the cause of the commotion, and putting his head between the flaps of the wagon-cover, saw a strange sight. They seemed to be in camp in the middle of a lake; the water was nearly up to the wagon-body, and still rising, while Rawlins' horse was almost swimming!

There was no time to lose, and without a moment's hesitation Youngblood jumped into the ice-cold water up to his waist, hitched up the team, and got them under way.

It took them nearly half a day to get out of their delightful camp, and, to use Youngblood's own words, "it was a trying time for us poor sinners. I don't know which is the worse, and I have experienced both—too much water or too little."

20

CHAPTER XXVIII.

YOUNGBLOOD AS A PISCATOR—O'BRIEN THE
HUSTLER—YOUNGBLOOD, JUNIOR, WINS
HIS SPURS—A MODERN ANANIAS—OUT-
WITTING THE REDS.

After having gotten safely out of their
Slough of Despond, our friends steered their
schooner for a point about twenty miles distant, where a new town had been laid out
only a few weeks. before. Upon arriving at
their destination, they found a house to be
sure, but not the slightest vestige of a town,
as the sole building was occupied by Mr.
Nick Whitsee, a carpenter, who was monarch
of all he surveyed, and did the honors of the
one-storied metropolis in a very hearty manner.

While waiting for the night to come, and
anticipating the satisfaction one feels in
striking a comfortable place to sleep after
having passed through severe hardships,

Youngblood and his friend were surprised
at the arrival of two more unfortunates
upon just such an errand as theirs. It
seems that they also had been caught in the
storm, being encamped on a small branch
near the dry (?) lake which our hunters had
congratulated themselves upon finding, and
when the down-pour came, away went tent,
grub, and, in short, everything that could
float, and although they chased their traps
ten miles or more down-stream, they were
rewarded only by their labor for their pains.

Their misadventure necessitated a change
in the plans of our hunters, who were obliged
to put back to Rawlins' ranch for repairs
and supplies, and when they reached his
hospitable abode, life again seemed worth
living. Youngblood's son was so worked up
over the description of their fun (?) that he
was very anxious to take his father's place
on the next trip, and the latter was only too
glad to send a substitute, thinking that he
could put in his time to good advantage with
the hook and line, and in getting the rest

which usually accompanies such a holiday.
The hunting party was reinforced, just before
starting, by a Mr. Keys, who "could stand
anything," but who gave up in disgust after
they had gone about eighty miles, leaving
Rawlins and Youngblood, junior, to continue
the search for calves, but with no immediate
satisfactory results.

In the meantime, our hero was taking fish
in great numbers, and, consequently, life
easy.   The location of his fishing-ground
was on the divide between Farwell, Texas,
and a new town which at that time was not
old enough to possess a name, but which
has since then undoubtedly been christened,
and by this time must be thriving, as the
location is a good one.   The chief citizen
was a Mr. O'Brien, and he was a "hustler"
from head-waters.   He didn't have time to
fish, but about three times a day did manage
to stop "booming" long enough to make
Youngblood's string look as though it had
supplied a whole regiment of famished men.
This O'Brien was the typical Western man

of enterprise. If you couldn't use the land for farming or building purposes, his assurance that it was "good to eat on bread" secured the customer and closed the trade!

While Youngblood was coaxing three-pound trout from their hiding-places, O'Brien was on the jump, preparing for the arrival of thirty-three families of Dunkards that were on their way to this point, and, of course, he "got there with both feet."

The place seemed to be quite a stamping-ground for the followers of Izaak Walton, and one old gentleman named Murphy, who had stopped for a few minutes to look on, remained two days enjoying the amusement.

While the father was having fun with the finny tribe, the son had struck pay-dirt, having run across a herd of buffalo with which there were some calves. The boy had much of the spirit of the father in him, and, dashing into the bunch, secured one calf (which was quite young) with little difficulty; but one frisky young bull led him a lively race for about five miles, and had he not been well mounted, he might have been "taken into camp" himself instead of being the captor, for the moment he reached over from his cayuse and caught the calf by the tail, the brute set up the most unearthly bellow, which brought Mrs. Buffalo down upon them, head and tail up, like a hog in a corn-field. For a moment it looked serious for the young fellow, as it is not a pleasant sen-sation to feel that you are the chief attrac-tion for an infuriated beast, and a thousand pounds of live buffalo-meat was coming for him for all there was in the game. But the boy was nervy, and did not for a moment think of dropping his prize; so, pulling his revolver, he fired, fortunately breaking the fore leg of the cow, which put her out of the race, and, subsequently, her hide in the wagon.

These two calves were all our friends suc-ceeded in capturing, for, although they hunted far and wide, no more were seen, and for the first time they began to realize that the noble buffalo is practically extinct.

Youngblood says that there are but comparatively few left out of the millions that have ranged on the plains, and instead of seeing the earth black with these mighty brutes, as he has seen it, a bleached skull here and there is about all that is left. Civilization has driven them the way of the red-skins, and instead of hearing the thunder of their hoofs on the prairie, the noise of the reaper greets the ear, and the sun of progress dispels the mist of romance with which the magic pen of Fenimore Cooper had enveloped the West.

Owing to this scarcity, Youngblood found himself compelled to fall back upon his old love—antelope. They had been having altogether too happy a time of it, and to remind them that he had not quite forgotten them, after his long rest, he made up his mind to set out for a likely place which he knew of near the head-waters of the north fork of the Cimarron River, and about thirty miles south of the beautiful and prosperous town of Lakin, which place he designed to make his headquarters. He took his four boys along with him, as this was to be merely a business trip. They had four wagons, and hoped to make a couple of trips out of Lakin before the weather drove the antelope to the far south.

On a lovely morning they started. The weather—bright and glorious—seemed to put new life into the party as it bowled along over the smooth prairie, with the prospect of plenty of game ahead, as, from all reports, antelope had been seen in large quantities within twenty miles, right on their track. They had bought two new horses in Lakin, both of which proved to be magnificent animals—one of them especially, which they afterward used in the saddle, and found to be a "hummer." The boy Jim named her "Dame Trot," and claimed her as his own, which Youngblood generously allowed, as the boy loved a good horse, and knew one when he saw him. Just before they pitched camp for the night, Youngblood took a good look round, as usual, and about five miles

straight ahead, near the Cimarron River, he
spied a solitary buffalo standing on a high
bluff.   This was too much for him, so he
took the freshest horse he had, and taking
advantage of a dip in the prairie to the left,
rode within 400 yards without being seen,
dismounted, and at 300 yards tried a shot at
the buffalo's hump, which, from the lay of
the land, was about all he could see.   It was
a lucky shot, and the bull dropped, startling
the rest of the herd, which numbered five,
toward the river.   For the first day out, this
was not so bad, and had Youngblood not re-
sisted the temptation to further test his
marksmanship, might have been better.
When he got back to camp he found a man
there who was out for game, and who had been
attracted by the shots in the direction of the
camp.   Youngblood had brought the hump
of the buffalo along, and was fortunately in
a position to play the host to advantage.
While supper was being prepared, two of the
boys went after the meat which had been left
behind.   The stranger was a great talker,

and a very Nimrod withal, and to him Youngblood was indebted (?) for many practical
hints and much information in. regard to
hunting, which, to a tenderfoot, would have
been most edifying. He mentioned Mr.
Youngblood's name as that of a great hunter,
and told how many buffalo they had killed
together; which, considering the fact that
our friend had never seen this modern
Ananias before, was not without its point.
However, he left him to enjoy his narrative
undisturbed. He said that he had that
morning passed a party of four gentlemen,
amateurs in the profession, who were footing
it to Lakin, having had their horses stolen by
a party of Indians from the south, who had
ventured to defy the proprieties and run the
risk of trouble with the authorities. This
was unpleasant news, as our party had stock
to lose, and it behooved them to be on the
watch, as it had happened only a few miles
beyond the Cimarron River.

The next morning Mr. Stranger went his
way, and Youngblood and his party pulled

out for the south. They crossed the river in the afternoon of that day, without seeing any game. As soon as they had passed the river and reached the top of the bluff bordering it, they could see a light smoke ahead of them, invisible to an unpracticed eye, which might mark the camp either of the Indians or of the disgruntled amateurs, though they feared, from the looks of the smoke (which was evidently from a fire of well-dried wood), that the Indians were there, and that their neighbors were unpleasant ones.

Next morning, an hour after sunrise, they were on the road, and soon reached a good camp. Taking his son, who was a credit to his teacher, Youngblood rode toward a well-wooded bluff marking a bend in the river, in search of game, and soon sighted a large herd of antelope making for them. Concealing their horses as best they could, the hunters laid down, facing the wind and the antelope, which kept on straight toward their hiding-place at such speed as indicated that they had scented something. On they

came, and were soon within thirty yards,
when our friends, each singling out his shot,
fired, getting two at the first volley.   At
sound of the shot, the herd stood stock still,
and before it broke away to the left they
had two more, and three more fell from four
flying shots, leaving Youngblood well satisfied, and the boy delighted at the good work
they had done.   As agreed, the boys from the
camp were soon on hand with a team, and
the executioners went on ahead after more,
but all day without success.

That night they were startled by the neigh-
ing of the horses, and at once thinking that
Indians might be around, Youngblood started
up to satisfy himself that the stock were
all right.   He found Dame Trot, but could
see nothing of the others, and gave them up
for lost.   The Indians were evidently hard
cases, and poor neighbors to have around; so
sending one of the boys out next morning on
their trail to keep them in touch, Youngblood started off on foot for the nearest town
to get horses.   He had some trouble in secur-

ing what he wanted, but in a couple of days succeeded in getting three that pleased him. They were fine, strong animals, that had not done much work. After warning the settlers to be on the lookout for the Indians, Youngblood started back for camp, and had not gone ten miles on his journey before he met his son, who had ridden out to meet him with the news that he had succeeded in recovering all the horses, and getting clear away before the Indians got a chance at him. It was lucky that Youngblood had brought out two old hunters with him, which he had done as a measure of precaution, thinking it best to strengthen the party as much as possible. All haste was made back to camp, where everything was found quiet and undisturbed, although they felt sure that the Indians must be still sneaking around.

It seems that Youngblood, junior, had ridden out on the trail of the Indians after leaving camp, and had managed to keep out of their sight until about noon, when he sighted their camp-fire, and carefully creeping up as near as he could with safety, within range of a good field-glass with which he had supplied himself, he made out that something unusual was going on. The Indians all appeared to be asleep under the shelter of their tepees of branches of trees and grasses, for the day was very warm for the season of the year— all except one, a sentry, who sat nodding on his bronco, and evidently much more interested in a familiar-looking object which he held in his hand, and appeared to use as a trumpet at frequent intervals, than in his duty. It was hard work blowing into this instrument, as he seemed to get very weary over it, and finally sliding to the ground, he appeared to have got through with his sentry duty, as he made no sign thereafter.

Our young hunter suspected that the object of his attentions was a bottle, and, emboldened by appearances, crept up closer and closer until within 100 yards, where he lay at the edge of his cover cogitating over the situation. The fire-water had been too much for the "reds," who lay oblivious to every-

thing, perhaps dreaming of their happy
hunting-grounds—evidently, from the number of the slain (in bottles), safe from all
trouble and care for some time to come.
The boy made up his mind that he would
risk it, feeling certain that the awakening
would not be yet, and try to secure the
horses, which were picketed close by the
camp; so walking boldly up, it was but the
work of a moment to cut the tethers, leap on
the back of the best of the horses, and run
for it. The Indians never moved, and the
victor rode into camp leading the spoils
behind him. This was too much like old
times, so a council was at once called, at
which it was decided to send the two
youngest boys back to Lakin, and keep on
the hunt without them.

Next day, with the help of the two
recruits, our party got ten antelope, and
started the boys off with one wagon and a
small load, and with Youngblood, junior, for
an escort on "Dame Trot." The following
afternoon the young man was back, having

seen his convoy into safety without accident or anything important to report. The Indians had evidently left for parts unknown, doubtless alarmed at the size of the party and Master Youngblood's way of doing things; consequently they heard no more of them for several weeks, though they kept a good lookout, and ran no risks with their live stock.

During the next two weeks antelope were so plentiful that our party got over 200 of them, and finding sport so good, made a business of drying the meat and salting down the hides, until they had all they could carry, when the party turned head toward Lakin, at which point they disposed of their spoils to good advantage, and laid off for a few days' rest which they had so fully earned.

CHAPTER XXIX.

A NEW EDITION OF THE ONE-HORSE SHAY—
A MIGHTY HUNT—A NEEDLESS SCARE—
"VENGEANCE IS MINE," SAITH THE PIO-
NEER—A SCRIMMAGE WITH LO VERMIN.

A life of idleness seemed wholly unfitted
for Youngblood, who, after remaining a few
days in Lakin, was approached by a couple
of men from Pennsylvania, who were very
anxious to have him secure a bunch of wild
horses for them. This was an undertaking
which our alert friend was most willing to
join in; so he started on a tour of exploration, returning with the information that
he had discovered a band of twenty-seven.
The gentlemen from the Keystone State at
once engaged him to bring them in, and our
hunter started—this time in a buggy, for a
change. This luxurious method of traveling,
however, was not kept up long; for the first
day out, and while feeding his team (not

having time to unharness), a veritable whirl-
wind struck the outfit, hoisting a buffalo-
robe in the air and throwing it on the horses,
evidently much to their disgust, for when
they were through kicking there was not
enough of the buggy left to even carry the
monument the city of New York has been
so long erecting to the memory of General
Grant!

This certainly was not an agreeable thing
to have occur; but Youngblood was out
for horses, and horses he proposed getting;
so improvising a saddle from the fateful robe,
he went on his way, but *not* rejoicing.

Now, while a saddle of this description
is better—a *little* better—than the upper
stringer of a rail-fence, the wildest fancy can
not make it a Whitman; so Youngblood's
chase of fifteen days after the broncos was
a trying one for him; but he finally reached
their grazing-place.

To get these timid animals was the next
thing to be done, and all of our hero's
knowledge of their habits was brought into

play to bring about his success. The leader of the band was a magnificent black stallion with a perfectly marked star of white in his forehead, and for three days he proudly defied his would-be captor. He was finally "creased" by a single shot from Young-blood's Winchester, and when his haughty spirit had been broken by the hunter, he became the decoy that brought his harem and family into captivity.

It seems almost incredible that one human mind could accomplish the feat of capturing so many beasts at one time; but this Young-blood did, arriving in Lakin with the entire twenty-seven, and the would-be owners gladly handed him $280 for the bunch— making his three-weeks' jaunt quite a profitable one.

During the early summer, Youngblood made numerous excursions out of Lakin, with varying results, and in August found himself at Wallace, Kan., where rumors reached his ears that buffalo were quite plenty some distance to the northeast. Even

a rumor of such a state of affairs was sufficient to put him on the *qui vive;* so he
organized a party—five, including himself—
and determined to make a thorough search
for the game, being anxious to secure their
hides, which the slow but sure extinction of
the animals brought into good demand.

The party was fully equipped, and after
journeying for about 150 miles from Wallace,
meeting with only the usual adventures per-
taining to such a trip, they began to observe
signs of the game they were after, and one
day struck a large herd grazing near a forty-
acre corn-field connected with a lonely ranch.
Fire was immediately opened on the buffalo,
and then the fun began. The startled brutes
made for the corn-field breaking through
fences as though they were impediments of
straw, with the hunters in full pursuit, the
crack of their rifles resounding on every side,
and the pursuers yelling like Comanches.

Once among the waving corn, the shaggy
animals were doomed, their heavy bodies
being no match, in the soft ground, for the

light and wiry broncos ridden by our hunters, and the slaughter was immense, as when
Winchesters were empty, revolvers were
brought into use, and when the shooting
ceased the corn-field was as flat as though an
able-bodied cyclone had camped there, much
to the disgust of the owner of the ranch,
who saw in a few moments the work of his
season destroyed, as the corn was still in
the milk. A generous supply of fresh meat,
however, partially appeased him, and after
stripping the victims of their hides, the
hunters started toward Prairie-dog Creek,
near the edge of the settlement.

When the party drew in sight, the settlers
became much alarmed, and our friends could
see men running from the different cabins to
the largest one, each man carrying in his
hands a rifle, which flashed no pleasant welcome in the summer sun. They soon discovered that the new-comers were a party of
friends, and were overjoyed at the sight of
white men.

The cause of their previous actions was

soon learned. It seems that a band of red-
skins had been in the neighborhood the day
before, and had killed a lad of twelve whom
they met some little way from the settlement,
leaving his scalped and mutilated body to
the tender mercies of a broiling sun and
howling coyotes. This information caused
our party to reload their empty shells, with
a view to giving the red devils a reception
more warm than cordial, should they put in
an appearance.

After these preparations were made, the
hunters took the trail of the butchers, and
just before sundown found their deserted
camp, the cold ashes of their fires showing
that they had long since moved off. As an
evidence of the utter worthlessness of this
race, and to show their total lack of any sense
of obligation, our hunter found these noble
red men had left behind them to its fate a
poor, worn-out horse, whose body was covered
with cruel sores received in their service, and
now that, through their brutality, he was
useless, they would not spend a rifle-ball to

put him out of his misery, leaving him to be pulled to pieces by wolves when he fell from exhaustion, while they saved the leaden pellet which an all-wise (?) Government gratuitously supplies them, to use it against peaceable settlers! Surely, the Indian question is a vexatious one; but if the pioneers in the West were only let alone, they would settle it quickly. A rifle bullet is the only argument that appeals to these dirty outcasts, and their only permanent civilizer.

The suffering horse was put out of its misery, and our friends, leaving one of their number on sentry duty, rolled themselves in their blankets, and, with the starry heavens for ceiling, found that sleep which only tired men obtain.

Bright and early next morning a start was made, and, after going about ten miles, the sudden rising of two buzzards, and a hurried scamper of wolves from a clump of timber near, caused an investigation; and a horrible, but at the same time satisfactory, sight met the eyes of Youngblood and his friends;

for in the timber, and badly torn by wolves and buzzards, were the remains of three Indians, the stench arising from their decomposing bodies showing that they must have quit stealing and murdering about two weeks before, and the holes through each head—clean-cut in front and jagged in the back—showed that there was one white man, at least, who knew his business!

Leaving the dead carrion to its living prototype, our party moved off, and continued through the day to see signs of buffalo, which had undoubtedly been driven off by the Indians, the evidences of whose proximity were plenty.

Matters began to look ripe for a "scrap," and great caution was observed in camping that night; a sharp watch was kept, but no "reds" appeared, and one by one our party dropped off to sleep, with their loaded Winchesters beside them.

About sunrise, one of the party heard a noise, and, shielding his eyes with his hand from the rays of the rising sun, saw a band

of so-called braves, with their paint on, secreted behind a bank, near the edge of the timber. As he was about to raise an alarm, the well-known whiz of an arrow brought full consciousness to Youngblood, who awoke just in time to see an arrow strike the other hunter's extended hand, pinning it, cap and all, to his skull!

In an instant all hands were wide-awake, and the crack of rifles on one hand, and singing of arrows on the other, showed that both sides "had blood in the eye." But although there were at least four Indians to one white, the vermin (whose idea of a fight is to find a man with his back toward him) weakened at the first volley, and disappeared in the timber, taking with them four of their number who seemed badly hurt.

Owing to their numbers, and not knowing how badly his own party was injured, Youngblood did not think pursuit advisable, and turned his attention to his friends. The man who had discovered the band still had his hand (the left) pinned to his head, but dur-

ing the scrimmage had nervily worked his
gun to good advantage with the right, and
the imprisoned member was not released
until Youngblood pulled out the arrow, to do
which no small amount of force was necessary. Fortunately, the arrow was about
spent, or the bow sending it was a weak one;
otherwise another honest man would have
been made a victim of Uncle Sam's Indian
policy—or the lack of one. Finding the
injury comparatively trifling, Youngblood
continued his investigation, and was much
alarmed to find one of the party missing.
No one had seen him during the "scrap,"
and fear was felt as to his safety.

It was only after a repeated shouting of
his name, that a brush-heap a few yards
from camp seemed to move, and presently a
voice, as low as that which conscience is supposed to possess, was heard saying: " Youngblood! Ho! Youngblood, did you get 'em *all?*
Leave three for me any way;" and a pallid
face appeared in the center of the brush.
The situation was too ludicrous to admit of

any respect for the fear that belied his
words, and a yell of laughter greeted the
hero when he emerged from his hiding-place,
where he went, as he said, for the purpose
of ambushing the "reds;" but as he had
carefully left his gun behind, the assertion
must be taken *cum grano salis.*

The situation looked so squally that our
friends remained on the watch all day and
that night; but the Indians not appearing, the party moved off in the morning,
seeing, soon after their start, a man on foot
who made signals of distress to them.   They
at once approached, and found him to be
an old friend whose camp the Indians had
descended upon the day before, and after rob-
bing him of all they could take with them,
piled the balance of his goods upon his only
wagon, applied the torch, and fire soon
aided them in destroying everything that he
possessed, leaving 200 fine buffalo-skins to
rot.   Not content with this, the devils tied
him to a tree, placing meat and water just
out of his reach, and left him in that position,

to die a death of indescribable horror. He finally broke the thongs that bound him, and reached our party more dead than alive, and as perfect a picture of misery as one can meet.

As the loads were completed, and ammunition getting low, Youngblood determined to start for Wallace; so, taking their new-found companion, they proceeded on their way, meeting, at Beaver River, six men who had been outlawed for high crimes. These fellows wished our friends to join their party in a hunt, but of course they declined doing so. The outlaws were very hospitable, and begged so hard that Youngblood finally promised not to tell the authorities of their whereabouts, and again moved toward Wallace, reaching there in the midst of great excitement regarding Indians, who were supposed to have captured our friends, as they had been out forty-five days. But Youngblood laughed, and said he could stand the pressure as long as the red cusses. Selling his load of skins, he again took up the pipe of peace, which he lighted for a long smoke.

CHAPTER XXX.

For some time after the events recorded in the last chapter, Youngblood did but little hunting, feeling that he deserved a good rest, but on several occasions piloted people from the East on hunts for buffalo, much to their enjoyment, for many had never seen such big game, owing to the inability of their guides to find it; and the exclamations of surprise and delight, as animal after animal fell at Youngblood's fire, were the source of considerable entertainment to him.

Among other places visited was Garden City, founded by two old buffalo-hunting friends of Youngblood, who stuck by it through thick and thin, and finally have the pleasure of seeing in it one of the most thriving of the many like places that are growing up in the heart of a region where, a few years before, Youngblood had seen buffalo by the thousand, roaming over the rolling and flower-dotted prairie.

While at Wallace, a surveying party, bound for the " Panhandle " of Texas, came along, and their implements were a source of much curiosity to the settlers, who could not understand what the outfit meant. Youngblood, however, was too sharp to be fooled, and finally discovered, from the drift of their questions regarding the lay of the land, that they were out for the purpose of laying out an irrigating ditch, and, to aid them, our hero went to many localities with them. Among other points, Grenada, Col., was visited, and the party awakened much interest, but no one knew the truth, Youngblood having promised to keep silent for thirty days.

One night the party was nearly drowned out of a dug-out; and the wit of the company said: " Boys, let's go home. If *this* is a sample of the climate, we had better plant sponges than put our money into a ditch;" but as this rain-fall was most extraordinary, the surveyors were satisfied.

Youngblood kept the party in wonder, meat, and high spirits by his great marksmanship and good nature—one day knocking over a wolf that had the audacity to attempt the carrying off of an antelope from under their very noses, which our hunter had killed for supper.

Having taken this party over the desired route, and the scheme proving an undoubted success, Youngblood again started after buffalo, which were in great demand, and at one time, in his search for them, passed through a country in which for fifty miles there was not a drop of water except that which he carried in his own wagon. This necessitated his letting many good opportunities for buffalo escape him, as at such times water is more valuable than even food, as all know who have really felt the pangs of thirst. Finally a ranch was reached, and in reply to Youngblood's question as to whether there

22

were any buffalo in the neighborhood, the only occupant of the cabin tried to dissuade him from pursuing his journey; but when our friend starts for anything, he does not quit until he attains his object. When Mr. Ranchman tumbled to this fact, he admitted there might be some, which proved to be the case, for the next day Youngblood came upon a herd of about 600, out of which he got several, finishing his load in a few days; and on arriving at Coolidge he was gladly received, not only for himself, but for his load as well, as it was the first buffalo-meat seen in a long time—less skillful hunters not being able to get any.

It was now October, and, after a few days' rest, Youngblood decided to make another trip to the buffalo herd, and visit the taciturn ranchman as well. Upon arriving at his cabin, the latter was very anxious to make a trip. Taking him along, a herd of fifty was soon spied, and, by careful maneuvering on the part of Youngblood, four were secured, greatly to the wonder of the inexperienced hunter, who was so much excited over this (to Youngblood) common incident, that he couldn't help dress the slain, and probably has not wholly recovered up to this day.

A few more buffalo and several antelope made up the load, which was immediately gobbled up by the hungry inhabitants of Coolidge, who cried for "more" as lustily as Oliver Twist ever did.

To supply their demand, another start was soon made, Youngblood taking one of his sons with him this trip. The second day out, having met with no buffalo, the younger hunter became discouraged, and wanted to remain at Cimarron River for antelope. This he did, but Youngblood pushed on about twenty miles, and soon discovered, with the aid of his field-glass, two buffalo-cows, which he determined to have; but as the ground was a dead level, some sly crawling was necessary to the fulfillment of his desires. By this time the reader knows our old friend well enough to feel certain that those two

cows were in the wagon very shortly; and so
they were.

When watering his stock that night, just
before supper, wolves showed up in large
numbers, and the poison-box was again
brought into use, and in the morning six
large gray bodies that had once been wolves
were lying within a few rods of camp.
Youngblood took off their pelts, and sitting
down for a little rest, soon discovered five
large buffalo coming for water. When
they got in range he fired and wounded two.
But they started off in different directions,
and he was bound to have at least one.
Quick work was necessary, as the prairie was
on fire about six miles away, and coming
directly toward him. Another shot soon
dropped one of the bulls, and if ever the hide
came off a buffalo's back in quick time, it
was that particular skin, and tracks were
made to a point near the lake, where the
grass was so short that the fire would not
reach the spot.

There, Youngblood watched the flight of

the animals driven out by the fire, as they swept past; but the sight was not an un-usual one for him, so he turned in and slept the sleep of the healthy in body and mind, awaking early in the morning to find one of his mules missing, and, as luck would have it, the remaining one was a "bucker" of the worst sort; but he gave up his attempt to worry Youngblood off his back when he finally discovered that such a thing was an impossibility, notwithstanding his "bucks" and jumps, and went quietly along until the younger hunter was met, with whom our old friend returned once more to Coolidge.

Many such hunts were indulged in during the next few weeks, some being in snow-storms so dense that an object was hardly visible at the shortest distance. On one occasion, when about sixty-five miles out, the snow-fall was astonishing, covering the ground to a depth of from eight inches to three feet; and while Youngblood and his son were making the best time they could for a point of safety, the younger man discovered a single buffalo-bull, so covered with snow that he looked more like a pile of wool than an animated object. Youngblood, of course, must have him, even if he froze to death in the attempt, and finally threw his skin in the wagon, although the cold was so intense as to freeze it while it was being taken off. No wonder the West is a grand country, when men of this nerve abound!

Now and then would come a day in which a buffalo or so could be added to the load, which was finally completed, and "home again!" was the word. The cold continued intense, with heavy falls of snow almost daily, making the journey dangerous as well as difficult. Sometimes a drift would be struck that necessitated hitching the horses to the rear axle-tree to release the wagon, and one day the wheels stuck so firmly in a hole that two days were spent in digging them out. Thus it will be seen what hardships our two friends were called upon to meet and conquer. One of their most valuable horses fell on the ice one day, breaking his leg, and nothing but a shot from Youngblood's revolver put an end to its suffering. One of the wagons must now be abandoned. So, transferring the most valuable part of the load to the other vehicle, and making· a "spike team," they pushed their weary beasts with all the vigor possible toward Coolidge. Reaching Sisson's ranch, the welcome he offered was a veritable Godsend, and around his blazing fire they were told that they had been given up for lost, as many lives had been lost in the terrible weather. This gentleman's hospitality was fully appreciated; and after a night's rest, and with a present of a generous quantity of fresh meat, our friends again started on their weary journey home, crossing the Arkansas River on the ice, and reaching Coolidge, to find that the local paper had published an article to the effect that they had met death on the plains. While Youngblood has slept warm in snow a foot deep, it is too dangerous a practice to be indulged in, for death very often follows; and a couple of blankets in front of a blazing fire, in a comfortable house, is much to be preferred to the former manner of passing the night, all romances to the contrary notwithstanding.

About this time, so many investors wanted to see the country, that Youngblood made rather a business of acting as guide, in which he was engaged, with a friend named M. M. James, for about eight months; but his "hankering" for buffalo was too strong to be set aside, so he, with a man named W. Manghend, started to look some up. On their first trip they ran across a herd of nearly 200, out of which Youngblood alone got five, his "side partner" being too much surprised at the sight of the herd to do much more than stare at them. These, with a few antelope, were about all they wanted for that hunt, and they therefore started for Coolidge by way of Butte City; but the wolves annoyed them so during their first night that they were again obliged to have recourse to the poison-box, with the usual result.

When Youngblood reached Butte, the

town—made up of eastern men, chiefly, who had never seen a buffalo—turned out *en masse*, and the meat went like hot cakes. Many of the settlers at once started out on a little hunt of their own, determined to "do the old man up" by getting a big bull, freezing him, and standing him erect in the wagon, to show that Youngblood was not the only hunter in the section. But these enterprising individuals came back, after being gone five days, with their tails—so to speak—"between their legs," and it didn't seem as though much exertion was required to lift Mr. Buffalo into the wagon, as it turned out to be a jack-rabbit, and a one-eared one at that. The rest of the game consisted of a wall-eyed prairie-dog, killed probably with a stick; but they got so hungry for fresh meat that they had to eat him! After this failure they ceased attempting to take Youngblood's well-earned laurels from him.

Early in December, the people of Coolidge urged Youngblood to go and get them some

346 A MIGHTY HUNTER.

buffalo-meat for Christmas dinner; and, although the weather was cold and the days short, he was willing to inconvenience himself to accommodate them, and started out, returning with a good load on Christmas eve, amid much rejoicing.

A very singular incident occurred while he was out this time, which is worth relating. One day he struck a herd, and, after getting as close to them as he could, fired, causing one bull to stumble, but who immediately started off, but so slowly as to show that he was considerably hurt. Youngblood knew that he was all right, and so gave his attention to the others, killing one at the first fire, and then knocking another down, who immediately recovered his feet and charged, with "blood in his eye;" but our hunter didn't scare worth a cent, and, being well armed, soon put an end to the excited beast. In the meantime, the wounded bull had turned, and was stumbling along toward our friend, who could not imagine what made him use so peculiar a gait. Another shot stopped him altogether, and Youngblood found, upon examination, that the first bullet had put out both his eyes. .

But, as has been said, Coolidge was reached in good time for Christmas, the load being nearly 5,000 pounds of buffalo, several antelope, and twenty wolves; but the good people came near going hungry, as, just as he reached Butte City, Youngblood took a severe chill, owing to his hard work, and would not have eaten his Christmas dinner at Coolidge—or, perhaps, anywhere—had not Doctor Rickenbaugh, of Butte, used every effort, and finally brought him out of danger.

CHAPTER XXXI.

DREAMS GO BY CONTRARY—GAME PLENTIFUL
—PRAIRIES ON FIRE—A DUDE HUNTER.

After the holidays, Youngblood's sons
were very anxious to have him take them
for a little run through the "Panhandle,"
and, acceding to their request, he took two,
and the party started, reaching there after
an uneventful journey of four days. They
immediately began a search for buffalo, but
it certainly looked as if the animals had left
that part of the country, as it was thirteen
days before they saw a head. There were
about thirty in the herd, and, after all sorts
of maneuvers, Youngblood finally got within
range, and dropped three, the remainder
going off as though they had heard the crack
of Youngblood's rifle before, and knew what
it meant.

After dressing the fallen, our party made
after the runaways, but, although they fol-

lowed all day, did not see a hoof. Leaving their load at Cimarron River, our party started south again, and drove several days without falling in with any buffalo, although antelope were thicker than fleas on a dog's back. This amused the boys, but did not satisfy Youngblood, who was after larger game.

Camping that night on one of the tributaries of the Beaver River, one of the boys dreamed that buffalo were all driven from the country, and was greatly discouraged in the morning, feeling certain that his dream must be true, and that an empty wagon home would be the result, and could hardly believe his eyes when he saw, on a hill about a mile off, a herd of about fifty. A sharp chase resulted in the bagging of three, and the pursuit was continued after they had been dressed; but no more fell that day, and as it was very cold, and looked like snow, they looked about for a suitable place for camp.

While searching for a good spot, Youngblood, greatly to his surprise, ran across an old partner of his, named Lee Howard, of whom mention has been made before. This was a pleasant episode, as Howard is a fine fellow and a good hunter, and, if he so desired, could tell some interesting stories of his experience.

After spending a couple of days talking over old times with Howard, and taking advantage of several stray buffalo to increase the load, our party took up the line of march, passing through Boston, which had grown to be a lively town of great promise, and finally struck a spot that looked like buffalo; but it was four days before any turned up, and then it was only a single cow that was discovered lying down in the grass, and who saw the hunters as soon as they caught sight of her, and started off down a ravine at a lively gait. But Youngblood wanted her, and, leaving his sons in charge of the team, ran on foot for a cut about two miles off, to intercept the old lady. When he reached that point, he found, as had been expected, the cow grazing as quietly as though Youngblood was a thousand miles off instead of fifty yards, and when she realized her position, she only had time to select a soft spot to fall on, for down she dropped, and again Youngblood was master of the situation.

The wagon coming up shortly after, the cow was dressed and loaded, and our friends moved off to the left, soon discovering a large herd of Youngblood's pets, and plans were immediately laid to make a big haul. As our hunters were about to move on the herd, a band of wild horses galloped up, stampeding the buffalo, so that Youngblood and his party could get nothing but long, flying shots, but succeeded in bagging one elegant bull, notwithstanding.

Somewhat disappointed, but still hopeful, our friends proceeded on their journey, when their attention was attracted by a dark, moving mass on the horizon. As the land was perfectly level, the experienced eye of Youngblood soon discovered that a large herd of buffalo was rapidly approaching directly in their path. Getting the wagon and horses out of sight, Youngblood told the boys to stand ready, and when the big beasts passed, shortly after, about fifty shots were fired, and six fine animals concluded to go no further, while several others appeared to have felt the bullets.

The stock having had nothing to drink all day, and the nearest water being sixteen miles away, it was necessary to knock off hunting for the afternoon. The cause of the rush made by the buffalo was soon discovered to be a prairie-fire, and a lively one' at that, making the thirsty and tired horses work hard to keep ahead of it; but they succeeded in doing so, and reached the much-desired stream, almost wholly exhausted, about 2 o'clock in the morning. Never did confirmed toper more need or enjoy a drink than did Youngblood's faithful horses, and to say that they were carefully taken care of is a waste of words, for our old hunter knows too well the value of good horses to neglect them in the slightest degree.

Laying off the next day to rest, the follow-
23

ing morning they started bright and early, and reached Boston with their heavy load in the afternoon. Many strangers were there, among them being one who had heard of Youngblood's prowess in hunting, and who said that he never had and never would have believed his stories to be true, had he not seen the great load hauled in that day.

Our hero was approached by many strangers with requests for stories of his adventures, and he modestly and generously obliged them, staying up until late into the night— or rather early in the morning—before they would let him get the rest he had worked for, earned, and wanted to enjoy.

Disposing of much of the meat in Boston, but keeping plenty for his friends in Butte, who depended upon him, Youngblood started for the latter point the next day, where he was enthusiastically received. Here he ran across a young Englishman, named George A. Flett, of the British lager-beer trust, of Liverpool, who was a typical dude hunter —leather gaiters, single eye-glass, and all.

This gentleman had all sorts of hammerless guns, patent fishing-tackle, and all, and was going to astonish the natives with his prowess by field and flood. While the boys were unloading the wagon, he looked on in wonder, and some of his remarks were too good to be lost.

Jim had just thrown out a big jack-rabbit he had killed with a revolver, when Mr. Flett remarked to his friend: "Hi say, 'Arry, old boy, what a bloody big 'are hit his."

"Hare, nothing," said Youngblood, taking in Mr. Englishman at a glance. "That's a prairie-mole, and a small one, too; ain't it, Jimmy?"

"That's what!" remarked Jimmy, with a grin, helping to throw out a buffalo, which, when Mr. Flett saw it, caused him to remark: "Hi didn't know you 'ad Hangus cattle 'bout 'ere. But Hi say, 'Arry, what long 'air 'e 'as hon 'is 'ead!" and other ejaculations of a like order.

Our readers can rest assured that Young-

blood didn't spend much time over this typical English hunter (and murderer as well);
but we can feel certain that he would have
enjoyed having him along for one trip any
way.

After having supplied the wants of Butte,
our party proceeded to Coolidge, and turned
out the horses, as a reward for their good
work in time of need.

CHAPTER XXXII.

CONCLUSION.

Our narrative is finished, and there remains to be said but a few words to those whose kindly patience has followed our hero through these pages, necessarily incomplete and imperfect, as a man whose life has been such a busy and well-filled one has but little time to make accurate notes of all that occurred.

There is no apology to be offered or any explanation to be made for presenting this volume to the public, except that it was written at the request of many of Mr. Youngblood's friends, who, knowing of his life in the wild West, were anxious to have his adventures written and published exactly as they had happened.

There has been no attempt made at fanciful descriptions of imaginary adventures or a flowery style of narration, but it has been the intention to state only facts, and these in the briefest possible manner practicable; and if the reader does not consider this book sufficiently exciting or romantic, he must remember that it is not a dime novel, nor the life of a desperado, highway-robber, or murderer, but, as far as it goes, the true history of the life and adventures of an old hunter, a man of pure life and convictions, who at least has always tried to do his duty as he understood it, and who is devotedly attached to the wild prairie and woodland as God made them.

THE END.

COOLIDGE, KANSAS.

Coolidge, *the home of "A Mighty Hunter,"* has been referred to so many times in the preceding narrative, that perhaps some readers may have the curiosity, and others the patience, to read a few lines concerning this young City, for Coolidge is now a *full-fledged City*, the metropolis of Hamilton County and of Western Kansas. Although only a few years ago it was but a "trading-post" called Sargent, made up of an old sod fort and a flag station when the Santa Fé first went through, it now has about 1,500 bees, with the drones and moss-backs nearly all driven out, fine stone blocks, schools, and churches. The Peck Water-Works Company furnishes the City and the Railroad with the finest quality of water in the State, and a fire protection second to none. Its location, on the western line of Kansas, is almost identical with that of Kansas City on the eastern, and twenty years from now may find it as large a City; for its intermediately high altitude and one of the finest climates in the world (there having been only about forty stormy days in 1889, it being just near enough to the mountains to escape the storms of Eastern and Middle Kansas, and far enough away to avoid the cold from the snow in them), and its

l

Artesian Waters, possessing highly curative properties, are fast bringing Coolidge into prominence
as a *legitimate health resort.* Everyone recom-
mended to go to the mountains for pulmonary and
throat troubles will find it wise to stop here and
get acclimated. The change from a low altitude to
that of Manitou, Colorado Springs, and Denver is so
great that many well people can not stand it, while
invalids are often seriously injured, whereas if
they had acclimated themselves at Coolidge, they
would in most cases recover. The Artesian Water
has effected some *remarkable cures of chronic
kidney and liver troubles.* The address of those
cured will be promptly furnished on application.

Coolidge is situated on the Main Line of the
Santa Fé Railroad, which has here its Division
Round-house, Work-shops, and Eating-house, and
pays out monthly about $8,000. It is also situated
in the Valley of the Arkansas River, surrounded
by the most fertile lands in the West, and as a
stock-growing locality it is incomparable.

Youngblood, after having traversed the plains
for twenty years, here decided to pitch his tent,
finding here the best natural resources, climate,
and water, and knowing that a prosperous City
must eventually raise its walls in this favored spot.

All inquiries will be promptly and courteously
answered by the City Clerk, or the Coolidge State
Bank.

TESTIMONIALS.

This is to certify that I have known C. L. Youngblood 19 years, and want to say right here, that in all of my hunting on the plains I have never seen a better hunter. In fact, I believe that he has killed more game than any man that ever lived. This is saying a great deal, and a great many hunters will doubt this statement, but if they knew Charles Youngblood as I do, seen his hunting, been with him in camp, shared in his chases over the plains in pursuit of Buffalo, and been a helpmate to him in roaming over the plains after Mustangs, I think that their doubts would vanish. He is getting old now, but can yet kill more game than most men. The secret of his success is his skill in getting onto game; most hunters can shoot well, but getting close enough is the trouble. In getting onto game upon the level prairie (yes, level as floor for miles) is where most hunters are foiled. He has this down to perfection; he is a small man, but his wonderful endurance enables him to go farther after game than anyone that I ever saw. He is not given to boasting, says but very little about his exploits as a hunter; he is kind, hospitable, generous, and of good character; temperate in all his habits.

I want to say a word here in regard to his truthfulness and honesty. There is no man that I would believe quicker than him; no man that I would sooner trust. I will close these remarks by wishing him many blessings and happy years to come.

LEE HOWARD.

["Old Hunter Lee."]

NEWTON, KANSAS.

I do hereby cheerfully state that I have known Charles
L. Youngblood, "A Mighty Hunter," for the past sixteen
years. He is one of the most successful hunters I have
ever known or heard of on the Western plains, and I can
vouch for the truthfulness of his narrative.

J. H. BENDER,
Passenger Conductor on A., T. & S. F. R. R. Co.
for the past 17 years.

ATCHISON, TOPEKA & SANTA FÉ R. R. Co.
COOLIDGE STATION, Sept. 20, 1888.

I hereby recommend this book, written from the diary
of C. L. Youngblood, whom I have known in this section
of Western Kansas this past eight years. As "A Mighty
Hunter" and trapper he may have had equals, but excelled
by none.   Respectfully,

C. M. JOHNSTON,
Agt. A., T. & S. F. Ry.,
Coolidge, Kans.

ATCHISON, TOPEKA & SANTA FÉ R. R. Co.
COLORADO SPRINGS, July 1, 1889.

To whom it may concern: I have known Mr. C. L.
Youngblood since 1883. During the several years I was
agent at Coolidge, Kansas, the home of the old frontiers-
man, I shipped to Eastern markets large quantities of
Buffalo and Antelope killed by him. Mr. Youngblood is
our oldest living hunter on the plains; his mind is active,
and full of reminiscences of encounters with Red-skins and
wild animals.   PRESTON C. DOCKSTADER,
Agent Santa Fé.

The Montezuma Hotel,

A handsome structure of stone, is located at Las Vegas Hot Springs, New Mexico. This renowned mid-continent pleasure and health resort is six miles from the city of Las Vegas, on a branch of the

Atchison, Topeka & Santa Fé Railroad.

An elevation of 7,000 feet above sea-level; a bright and clear climate (ten sunny days for every cloudy one), and beautiful mountain scenery, with the attendant pleasures of hunting and fishing, combine to make Las Vegas Hot Springs deservedly popular among all classes of tourists.

Montezuma Hotel has every modern convenience, including telegraph, telephone, and four daily passenger trains. It is also open for guests

EVERY DAY IN THE YEAR.

The many springs near the hotel are justly celebrated for their healing properties.

Round-trip excursion tickets are on sale to Las Vegas Hot Springs at all principal coupon stations.

Write for pamphlet to

GEO. T. NICHOLSON,

General Passenger and Ticket Agent A., T. & S. F. R. R.,

TOPEKA, KANSAS,

Or, JNO. J. BYRNE, Ass't Gen'l Pass. and Ticket Agt., Chicago, Ill.

Ætna National Bank,

S. W. Cor. Twelfth and Main Streets,

KANSAS CITY, MO.

CAPITAL, - - - $250,000.00.

OFFICERS.

R. W. TUREMAN, President.

M. H. CRAWFORD, Vice-President.

L. D. COOPER, Cashier.

R. J. HAWKINS, Assistant Cashier.

DIRECTORS.

R. W. TUREMAN, E. K. SUMERWELL, T. B. BUCKNER, JOHN HALL, CHARLES STEWART, L. D. COOPER, JUDGE J. L. SMITH, R. E. TALPEY, DR. G. W. FITZPATRICK, J. K. RIFFEL, R. J. HAWKINS, H. S. RHODES, M. H. CRAWFORD, F. F. ROZZELLE, JUDGE A. W. ALLEN.